D1016951

Praise for *Chase Against Time*

"Edgy, suspenseful, and fun."
—Brad Turner
Producer and director, *24*

"Mystery, action . . . Chase Manning has it all. Fans of
Encyclopedia Brown are sure to love this series."
—Lee Edward Födi
Author of The Chronicles of Kendra Kandlestar

**Here's what some young mystery readers
are saying about *Chase Against Time*:**

"A sure winner! Impossible to put down!
Kids will devour this school day tale."
—Julio Escarce

"I have to say, this book has wonderful cliff-hangers."
—Sedona Culp

"An amazing story!"
—Grace Gordon

"*Chase Against Time* is a mystery that will
change the way you view the world."
—Bobby Butchko

CHASE

Against Time

CHASE
Against Time

Chase Manning Mystery #1

STEVE REIFMAN

Brown Books Publishing Group
Dallas, Texas

Chase Against Time

Brown Books Publishing Group
16250 Knoll Trail, Suite 205
Dallas, Texas 75248
www.brownbooks.com
(972) 381-0009

ISBN 978-1-61254-031-3
Library of Congress Control Number 2011942862

Printed in the United States of America
10 9 8 7 6 5 4 3 2 1

For more information, please visit www.stevereifman.com.

To Mom, Dad, Lynn,
Jeff, Sylvia, Alan, Ari, and Jordy.

To all the family, friends, teachers,
and students whose support, expertise, and
encouragement made this book possible.

Table of Contents

ACKNOWLEDGMENTS

I would like to acknowledge the terrific work done by the entire Brown Books team. You are all true professionals. It has been a genuine pleasure working with you.

I would also like to thank Andrew Hecht for doing such an outstanding job designing www.stevereifman.com.

Friday, March 26

CHAPTER 1

8:30 a.m.

Sensational job this morning, everyone. Sweet sounds all around. Tonight's concert will be absolutely fabulous. Please pack up your instruments and head back to your classrooms. My next group will be here in a minute."

"Oh, yeah, I forgot the little kids are coming in after us today."

"Victoria, dear, you realize, of course, that the members of the intermediate orchestra are only one year younger than you, don't you?"

"I know, Mrs. Washington, but they're just so young and immature."

Mrs. Washington ignored the sixth grader and slid back to her stand at the front of the auditorium to prepare for the crowd gathering outside the door.

I was one of the little kids waiting to get inside, and I had a lot on my mind.

"Chase, stop staring at that thing," my friend Skip said.

"I can't help it."

"It's just a cello."

Harold Buckingham—he preferred Skip—was right about most things. After all, they don't let just anybody move directly from kindergarten to second grade at Apple Valley Elementary. About the cello, however, he couldn't have been more wrong. A mere instrument, it wasn't. It was the key to making my lifelong dream come true.

"Chase, the cello's going to be in that entryway all day. Let's go. Rehearsal's starting in a minute."

Reluctantly, I pulled myself away from the cello and reached the auditorium door right when Victoria and the rest of her jubilant classmates in the Sixth Grade Honors Orchestra were about to exit. They could afford to be happy and carefree. They were about to graduate and didn't have to think about next year.

I was hoping Victoria would leave Skip and me alone when she saw us. She rarely did.

"Keep your head down," Skip suggested. "Maybe she won't see our faces."

No such luck.

"Well, if isn't Chase and Skip," she said haughtily.

"Uh, hi, Victoria," we simultaneously responded, hoping to keep the conversation short.

"Boys, are those really your names or just what you two like to do at recess?"

Without waiting for an answer, Victoria plowed her shoulders through ours and headed on her way. My eyes followed her down the hallway. Skip noticed.

"Chase, don't tell me that you *like* that girl."

"Don't worry. It's not her. It's her honors orchestra jacket."

"Well, stop staring at that thing. You'll get yours next year."

"I hope so."

8:37 a.m.

CHAPTER 2

8:38 a.m.

We walked inside to set up our rented instruments. Skip took a seat next to Amy Simmons with the rest of the viola players while I joined Jenny Gordon, my longtime neighbor and friend, and the other cellists across the room.

Jenny and I had been talking about playing together next year ever since we joined the beginning orchestra as fourth graders. If we made the advanced orchestra with most of our other classmates, it would be pretty cool.

But we had our eyes on a bigger prize.

The two of us were seeking a spot in next year's Sixth Grade Honors Orchestra. Only a select few of Apple Valley's musicians made it, and our opportunity was so close, we could practically taste it. The honors orchestra traveled to different performances, competed in the state music championship, and got to wear cool jackets, like the one I was staring at before. Believe me, I wasn't staring at Victoria.

Mrs. Washington and her committee didn't let just anybody into this group. We had to earn it. Today was the day we would try to do that.

"What time's your tryout later?" Jenny asked.

"Two forty-five," I responded. "When's yours?"

"Two."

"Settle down, everyone, and let's begin," Mrs. Washington instructed. "This morning's rehearsal will feature the three songs we will be performing at tonight's Spring String Thing before the dinner and auction start."

I must have heard the name of tonight's event at least a hundred times over the past couple weeks, but I still couldn't help laughing at it. "Who thought of that name?" I mumbled to myself. I didn't think anyone else could hear me.

"Shh!" Jenny shot back. "Amy's sitting right over there."

"So?"

"Her mom created that name."

"No offense, I know Amy is your best friend and all, but that's really not a very good name."

"I know, I know," Jenny whispered. "But Amy's

mom is the PTA president, and she's worked so hard on tonight's concert, dinner, and auction that nobody on the committee had the heart to say anything to her when she suggested it."

"Yeah, but 'Spring String Thing?' Isn't the idea of a name to get people to want to come to the event?" I teased.

"Very funny," Jenny responded. "Alice wanted a name that tied into the auction for the cello, and cellos do have strings, and right now is the beginning of spring, and . . ."

I decided not to push the issue any further. I could tell Jenny agreed with me and was just sticking up for her friend's mom. Jenny was always loyal like that, and I admired her for it.

Our first song was usually our best, but today we started off a bit shaky. Halfway through, Skip accidentally dropped his bow and Jenny was so startled that she jumped out of her seat and nearly hit her head on the ceiling.

I was glad to see I wasn't the only one anxious about tonight. It wasn't so much the thought of playing in front of a bunch of people that made me nervous. That I could handle. It was the thought of what would happen to our music program next year if the spectacular cello on display in the entryway didn't raise enough money at the auction to offset the budget cuts our school board recently announced.

After waiting my whole life to play cello for Mrs. Washington in the honors orchestra and to compete in the state music competition, I couldn't bear to think of having our entire instrumental music program eliminated. That couldn't happen at Apple Valley. Not now. The timing was too cruel.

Mr. Andrews, our principal, walked in smiling after we resumed playing. As he approached our teacher, he looked as if he had something to tell us.

"Mary, please forgive my interruption, but I know how concerned you and your students are about the prospect of losing our wonderful music program if we don't raise enough money at tonight's auction to make up for our budget shortfall."

"Yes, Mr. Andrews, it's definitely been on all our minds lately."

"Well, I believe I come bearing good news."

I sat up taller in my chair.

"Earlier this morning I received phone calls from three different local music collectors. They told me they were so concerned about Apple Valley losing its music program that they were planning to bid at tonight's auction so they could add the cello to their personal collections. In fact, they each said that they would be willing to spend enough money on it to save our music program. Now, I don't want us to get our hopes up too high, but after hearing from these individuals, I'm confident that Apple Valley's musical tradition will keep humming along for many more years."

Those words were music to my ears. Along with everyone else in the room, I let out a huge sigh of relief. Of course, I didn't want to get my hopes up too high, as Mr. Andrews said, but I also knew my principal was a cautious person and wouldn't have expressed confidence if he didn't really believe the music program was about to be saved.

"Wonderful news, Mr. Andrews," said Mrs. Washington. "Thanks so much for sharing it with us."

"No problem," the principal replied. "Kids, I think many of you know that I used to be a music teacher. I was pretty good at it, too, but you've got the absolute best music teacher in the state. Learn as much as you can from her. For seven straight years, her honors orchestra has won the state music competition, and this year's group seems like a shoe-in to make it eight. I'm confident our tradition will continue next year. Keep practicing. Good luck to those of you who are trying out this afternoon for next year's honors orchestra, good luck in today's raffle, and good luck tonight."

Once Mr. Andrews left, we only had a few minutes to ourselves before we heard a ruckus at the door.

"OK, kids, wait outside while I get the auditorium set up for class," Coach Turner said with his back to us. Then he turned around and noticed our rehearsal. "Hey, what are all of you doing in here? I always bring my PE class in here at this time."

"Hi, Coach," Mrs. Washington replied, "didn't you get the e-mail about today's special rehearsal schedule? I'll be using the auditorium until nine."

"I didn't get any e-mail," he grumbled. He turned to his assistant. "Did you get an e-mail?"

"No, Coach, I didn't."

"Let me get this straight, Mary. You're rehearsing for tonight's special event?"

"Yes, that's right."

"Let's see," he said, turning back to his assistant. "My basketball team made the playoffs last month. My track team wins gold medals every year at the city meet. And of course, my football team has won five league championships. But do they ever have any special events for my teams?"

"No, Coach, they don't," the assistant replied.

"Of course they don't!" Coach grumbled. "I've been here twelve years, and not once have they had a special event for one of my teams."

"It just doesn't seem fair," the assistant said.

"Of course it's not fair!" Coach barked. "But just because our little music program's in some trouble, they're putting on this special event. OK, kids, let's turn around and head back to the playground. It seems that once again music is more important at this school than physical education."

After the shock of Coach Turner's outburst wore off, we began our second song, but one person kept messing up during the same part.

Me.

The first time it happened Mrs. Washington just gave me a look. When I repeated my mistake thirty seconds later, she stopped class. "Chase, is there a problem?"

"No, Mrs. Washington."

"Are you feeling OK?"

"I haven't slept much this week, but I'm fine."

"Chase, I don't think any of us have slept well lately, but we need to clean up this part. You usually play it very well, but something seems to be off today. Be sure you find time today to work on it before your tryout and tonight's concert. Understand?"

"Yes, ma'am."

Our rehearsal ended a few minutes later. We played our last song perfectly and ended on a high note. Jenny gave me a puzzled look when she noticed the pink attendance sheet sticking out of my backpack.

"Hey, Chase," she said, "didn't Mrs. Kennedy want you to take that to the office before we came in here?"

"Oh, geez, you're right, I forgot all about it," I replied.

I quickly grabbed my stuff, said good-bye to everyone, and hightailed it to the office.

Being Student of the Week in Mrs. Kennedy's class was a sweet deal. You got to answer the phone, take the attendance sheet to the office, and deliver things to other classes. Each morning you stood outside the door and greeted the rest of the kids as they entered the room. Basically, if Mrs. Kennedy had a job that needed to get done, you got to do it. She also gave the Student of the Week a cool certificate and hung it on a bulletin board where you could put up pictures of your family and friends.

When I approached the entrance, nobody else was around. The hallways were completely empty and silent. I opened the door to the office, walked through the entryway, and saw Mr. Andrews and Mrs. Gonzales, the office manager, going over some paperwork.

I passed the glass display case, looked up to say hello to the adults, and then, realizing what I had just seen, came to a complete stop. Mr. Andrews and Mrs. Gonzales noticed my reaction and followed me back to the entryway. Immediately, we all looked at one another in disbelief.

The cello was gone.

9:06 a.m.

CHAPTER 3

9:07 a.m.

I had never seen Mr. Andrews that upset before. After the three of us realized the cello had been stolen from its display case, the principal's face turned dark red and he seemed ready to explode. After a few deep breaths, though, Mr. Andrews pulled himself together, sent Mrs. Gonzales to finish her paperwork, and asked me to come into his office.

I sat down in a chair across from the principal's desk just as Mr. Andrews slammed the door shut behind us.

"I can't believe that a student at this school would steal *anything*," Mr. Andrews fumed, "let alone something as important and as valuable as this cello. I just can't believe this has happened. I mean, the kind folks down at the Apple Valley Community Orchestra were concerned enough about our music program to donate a beautiful, handcrafted cello once played by the world-famous Yo-Yo Ma, and now it's gone. What in the world am I going to tell them?"

I didn't have a good answer for him. It hurt to see Mr. Andrews in such anguish.

"Chase, we have to get to the bottom of this."

"*We*, sir?" I responded.

"Yes, we. I need your help. All of the PTA parents, music boosters, and orchestra alumni will be here soon for a bunch of meetings and ceremonies leading up to tonight's event. I'll be with them the whole day, and there's no way I'm going to have any time to investigate who might have taken the cello."

"You'd like *me* to investigate for you?" I asked, shocked by this request.

"Yes, I would. You see, Chase, I trust you. You have a terrific reputation. I know how you feel about music. I also know that your older brother and sister each won state championships at Apple Valley. I know how badly you want to follow in their footsteps next year in the honors orchestra."

"Yes, sir. Thank you, but do you really think I should be the one trying to solve this crime?"

"You're the perfect person to solve this crime. Listen, nobody else can know about this. If the parents, or teachers, or even the other students find out what just happened, there will be panic everywhere. I need you to find out who did this, and I need you to do it without mentioning that the cello's been stolen."

"But Mr. Andrews, don't people usually call the police when something like this happens? Shouldn't we do that instead?"

"Calling the police will raise too many questions and lead to panic. We can't afford that right now."

"But, sir, I really don't—"

"Chase, my mind is made up. You're my man. I know you can do it. Hold on a second. Mrs. Gonzales," Mr. Andrews said, pressing the intercom button to get her attention, "may I see you for a moment, please?"

Mrs. Gonzales entered the principal's office and shut the door.

"Mrs. Gonzales," Mr. Andrews began, "nobody else can know about this theft. I don't want the whole school in a panic. Chase is going to investigate for me while I'm with the PTA and our other visitors today, and I'd like you to give him whatever help he needs."

"Yes, sir," she replied.

"Another thing," he said, "I want you to take a piece of the large poster board we have in the workroom and use it to cover the glass display case in the entryway. That way nobody else will see it empty."

"Yes, Mr. Andrews, I'll do it right away. Is there anything else?" she asked.

The principal didn't respond immediately. He put his hand on his head and thought for a moment. Then he said, "Actually, there is. When people see the blank sign, they're going to wonder why it's covering the glass. Write the following message on the sign: 'Cello Unveiling at Tonight's Spring String Thing.' Also, add a reminder that there's still time to buy tickets to the event to support this most worthy cause."

"Yes, sir," said Mrs. Gonzales. She returned to her desk.

I wasn't sure about all this. While the principal was giving his instructions to Mrs. Gonzales, I had developed a bad feeling in my stomach. Of course I wanted to help however I could, but should I really be the one in charge of finding the cello? I needed to speak up.

"But Mr. Andrews," I said, "I don't even know where to start. Are there any suspects you think I should investigate?"

Mr. Andrews leaned forward, put his elbows on his desk, and looked me right in the eye. "As much as it pains me to say to this about kids from my own school, I have to be honest with you. I have reason to believe the thief is one of three students. Now let me tell you their names and why I think they might have done this evil act."

Mr. Andrews then went on to tell me the names of the suspects and their possible motives. The first two names did not come at all as a surprise to me, but the third one certainly did.

As I was still reeling from hearing that third name, Mr. Andrews gave me my final instructions.

"Chase, I want to emphasize to you one last time how much we are all counting on you to recover the cello for us—and to do it without saying a word about how it was stolen this morning or how you're working with me. And one more thing: you have to solve this crime by 3:00 p.m. today. Once school gets out, you know, it's spring break. All the after-school activities have been canceled, everyone will be gone for two whole weeks, and there will be no way to track down the thief."

I then stood up, left the office, and walked slowly back to class. I sure hoped the thief was one of the first two names Mr. Andrews gave me.

I didn't want to have to investigate that third name.

9:18 a.m.

CHAPTER 4

9:19 a.m.

I was almost halfway back to class when I stopped and thought some more about the three names Mr. Andrews gave me. I closed my eyes, dropped my chin to my chest, and began to focus my mind on the task at hand.

Dave Morrison was an obvious suspect. He was Apple Valley's only true bully. Most of the kids tried to stay away from him and his temper whenever they could. The funny thing was, Dave actually liked music and was looking forward to playing in the advanced orchestra next year. But last week Mrs. Washington told him that because of his history of poor behavior, he wouldn't be allowed to join. That news really set him off. It was easy to see why Mr. Andrews thought Dave could have been the one who stole the cello. Revenge is a powerful motive.

Brock Fuller was another likely suspect. As a sixth

grader, earlier this year Brock played in the advanced orchestra and on the football team at the same time. There were many instances, however, when Brock's after-school music rehearsals conflicted with his after-school football practices, and he chose to go to football practice every time—even though he still wanted to be in the orchestra.

Mrs. Washington reached the point where she made Brock choose one or the other. Brock didn't want to make that choice and said he still wanted to do both. She became so frustrated with his constantly choosing football over music that she dismissed him from the orchestra.

Brock didn't take this news well. He tried arguing with Mrs. Washington, but she wouldn't budge. Finally, he stormed out of the music room, yelling, "Coach Turner was right. Music is a waste of my time. Who needs you? I like football ten times better anyway." Again, with a comment like that, it was easy to see why Mr. Andrews suspected Brock.

I didn't believe for a second that the third suspect could possibly be guilty, and I didn't want to spend one moment thinking about it. Instead, I had some decisions to make. I had to figure out how to talk privately with Dave and Brock, which one to talk to first, and, most important, how I would investigate them without letting on about the theft. On top of all that, I had to find a way to practice that tricky cello part before my tryout at 2:45 p.m.

I finished gathering my thoughts, opened my eyes, and continued back to class. Before I could look up, I felt my body crash into another student—a large one.

It was Brock Fuller.

"Dude, watch where you're going!" Brock grumbled as he continued walking down the hall.

I had to think fast. I couldn't let Brock get away because I knew there was no way I would have another chance like this to talk to him one-on-one.

"Hey, Brock, I'm really looking forward to playing in the orchestra next year," I said. I didn't know why I said it. They were just the first words that came to mind. I was nervous, and my nerves were making me act a little dorky. Rather than fight it, I began to think that dorkiness might actually be a good investigation strategy to use with Brock, even though none of the detectives on the TV shows I like to watch ever used that strategy.

"Dude, what are you talking about?" Brock replied, as if talking to me was a waste of his time.

I was determined to keep the conversation going.

"Hey, didn't you play in the advanced orchestra this year? Wasn't it great? Wasn't it the best?"

Brock took a step closer to me, and we were face-to-face—well, almost face-to-face. Brock had me by a good six inches and at least twenty-five pounds. "Dude, did you just ask me if music was great?"

"Yeah, wasn't it the best?" I repeated, shaking a little bit in fear.

"Dude, you know I was kicked out of the orchestra. You know I told Washington how I liked football better than music. Everybody here knows that story."

"Oh, that was *you*, Brock?" I asked. "I did hear that story about someone, but I didn't know it was you. I must be all mixed up." I was acting dorkier than I ever had.

As I got dorkier, Brock got angrier. Then the sixth grader began to mock me. He threw his hands up in the air, sarcastically singing, "Oh yeah, dude, music's so great. Music's the best."

Then, I saw it.

When Brock's hands were straight up in the air, a large cast emerged as his loose sweatshirt sleeve fell down to his elbow. The cast covered Brock's entire forearm and wrapped around his hand between his thumb and index finger. I also noticed a splint on the index finger of Brock's other hand.

"What happened to your arm and finger?" I inquired.

"Dude, I don't know why I'm even telling you, but I got in a skateboard accident yesterday. I broke my arm and sprained my finger."

"I'm sorry to hear that," I said, hoping that my sympathy would stop making Brock so angry with me.

Instead, Brock got even angrier and stepped closer to me. "Look, dude, I don't know what your deal is, but I've wasted enough time talking to you. Now I need to get back to class."

Having noticed the cast and splint, I concluded that Brock couldn't possibly have opened the display case and taken the cello earlier. Because the accident happened just yesterday, Mr. Andrews probably hadn't seen Brock this morning and couldn't have known that he could be ruled out as a suspect.

I wanted nothing more than to let Brock continue on his way, but I had to get one last piece of information. Putting my own safety on the line, I called out, "Hey, Brock, one more thing."

"What now, dude?" Brock said.

"Who's the Student of the Week in your class this week?"

"Dude, why do you care?"

I couldn't tell Brock the truth. I couldn't divulge that the second suspect, Dave Morrison, could only have stolen the cello if he was the Student of the Week in Brock and Dave's combined fifth- and sixth-grade class and had taken the attendance sheet to the office earlier that morning. That would have put Dave at the scene of the crime near the time of the theft.

But I had to answer Brock. "I'm the Student of the Week in my class, and I was just wondering who it was in yours."

"Dude, I don't have time for this. Leave me alone, won't you?"

"*Please*, Brock, just tell me. I have to know." I was practically begging at this point.

"Fine, I'll tell you, but after I do, you better stay away from me from now on. I mean it, dude. You come within ten feet of me and there's going to be trouble."

I gulped.

Brock hesitated for a moment. Then he said, "The Student of the Week in my class is Dave Morrison."

9:31 a.m.

CHAPTER 5

9:32 a.m.

I tried sneaking back into class as quietly as I could, but Mrs. Kennedy was waiting for me. For twenty-seven years Judy Kennedy had been a legend at Apple Valley. Her classes always worked hard, behaved well, and learned a ton. I was the third member of my family that she had taught. Interestingly, both my brother and sister were in her class as fifth graders, the year before they joined the honors orchestra and won state championships. I wanted that pattern to continue.

I shot her my best smile.

She shot me back her best teacher look.

"Chase, you're over twenty minutes late returning from rehearsal. What took you so long?"

"I'm sorry," I said. "Mr. Andrews wanted to talk to me about something, and he wanted me to do something for him."

"For that long?" she said.

"Yes."

Mrs. Kennedy gave me another look. She hesitated for a minute, but then gave me the benefit of the doubt.

Mrs. Kennedy wasn't a mean teacher. Tough, but fair. The two of us got along well, and she and my mom had been friends for years. Mrs. Kennedy had been to our home on many occasions, and my mom had been a regular classroom volunteer every time Mrs. Kennedy had a student named Manning on her roster.

Finally, she let me off the hook. "OK, why don't you sit down and get started on your math?"

I thanked Mrs. Kennedy, grabbed my math papers, and went to sit next to Jenny. She had already completed the first three problems.

"What's going on?" she whispered.

I knew I wasn't supposed to tell anybody about the theft, but I had already decided I was going to tell Jenny. For one thing, I knew I could trust her. For another, I thought she could help me with my investigation. She could be pretty clever sometimes.

"You have to promise to keep what I'm about to tell you a secret," I whispered.

"OK, I promise."

"No, really, Jenny, this is big. You need to promise not to tell anybody."

"Really, I promise."

"OK, when I went to take the attendance sheet to the office, I discovered that the cello had been stolen from the display case."

"What?" Jenny blurted out.

"Shh!" I commanded.

Mrs. Kennedy gave us a stern look before returning to her papers.

"Sorry," whispered Jenny. "I just wasn't expecting anything like that."

I then went on to tell her that Mr. Andrews and Mrs. Gonzales were the only other people who knew about the theft and that the principal had asked me to investigate and find the cello by 3:00 p.m. I also told her about my meeting with Brock.

"Who are the other suspects Mr. Andrews told you about?" Jenny asked.

"Since it couldn't have been Brock, Mr. Andrews thinks it's probably Dave Morrison."

"What about the third name?"

"Let's figure out how I'm going to investigate Dave first," I suggested. "If it turns out that he didn't do it, then we'll talk about the last suspect." I was happy with how that sounded. I was hoping with all my might that Jenny wouldn't push me to tell her that third name. I really didn't want to have to do that.

But Jenny wasn't going to let me off the hook so easily. "Come on, Chase, just tell—"

Luckily for me, right then the phone rang.

"Hang on," I said. "I have to get that."

I got up, answered the phone, and then walked over to Mrs. Kennedy to give her a message from Mrs. Gonzales in the office.

When I returned to Jenny, I said, "Oh, now where were we? Oh, yeah, you were about to help me figure out how I'm going to talk to Dave."

"I was?" asked a surprised Jenny.

"Yes. I have to figure out a way to leave class to talk to Dave. And I have to do it without getting Mrs. Kennedy upset. I've already been late once today, and I don't want to make her suspicious of me."

Jenny and I both sat quietly, thinking. Slowly, our attention found its way to the math problems. After about ten minutes, just as I was beginning to wonder if I'd ever get to investigate Dave, Jenny's face lit up.

"I know!" Jenny beamed. "Hold on, I'm going to get my cell phone."

"What?" I replied. "What are you doing with a cell phone in school?"

"It's really only for after school," she admitted. "You

know, if my ride is late or if I need to call my parents about something."

"Oh."

Before I knew it, Jenny had made her way to the closet in the back of the room where we kept our backpacks. Without Mrs. Kennedy noticing, Jenny knelt down, grabbed the cell phone from her backpack, and began punching in a number.

By closing my eyes and straining my ears, I could barely make out her side of the conversation.

After waiting a bit for someone to answer, Jenny took a deep breath, and in the most mature voice I had ever heard her use, she said, "Hello, I'm sorry to bother you, but I'm Jenny Gordon's aunt. Could you please ring Mrs. Kennedy's room and tell her that Jenny's mom will be fifteen minutes late picking her up today? I don't want the sweet little dear to worry when she doesn't see her mom at three o'clock."

She was calling the school!

Jenny didn't seem to get the response she wanted, and a look of concern appeared on her face. Thinking quickly, Jenny started repeating what she had just said.

"Uh, yes, could you please ring Mrs. Kennedy's classroom and tell her that Jenny Gordon's mother will be fifteen minutes late picking her up today? I don't want the sweet little dear to worry."

A short time later, she smiled and exhaled deeply.

As a relieved Jenny snuck back into her seat, I asked, "What was that all about?"

"Just hang on a second," she told me.

Sure enough, before I could muster a response, the phone rang again.

"Boy, we sure are popular today, aren't we?" Mrs. Kennedy joked.

I was beginning to get the picture as I walked to get the phone.

"Hello, student speaking," I said as I lifted the receiver.

"Hello," said Mrs. Gonzales, "could you please tell sweet little Jenny Gordon that her mom will be here to pick her up at three fifteen today?"

"Sure, no problem," I said, holding back a smile. I then gave Jenny a look and walked up to Mrs. Kennedy.

"Yes, Chase," my teacher said, "who was that?"

"Mrs. Kennedy, that was the office. Mr. Andrews needs me to finish doing what I was doing before. Hopefully it will only take a few minutes."

"OK, Chase, but hurry back. We're studying a critical math concept, and you've only been working on your paper for a short time."

"Yes, Mrs. Kennedy."

Technically, everything I said was true. That was the office calling, and Mr. Andrews did need me to continue with what I had started doing. It was very important to me to maintain my integrity while I investigated. I was trying to find a dishonest thief, and I refused to stoop to that person's level in order to do it. I was determined to catch the thief, and I was just as determined to do it as honestly as possible.

As I left the classroom, I thought about how brilliant Jenny's cell phone stunt was. I truly believed now that Dave Morrison had taken the cello. At least, I hoped he had.

I really didn't want to have to tell Jenny that third name.

9:55 a.m.

CHAPTER 6

9:56 a.m.

I walked upstairs to Mrs. O'Connor's class and mentally prepared to knock on the door and ask to speak to Dave Morrison. Before I did, though, I wanted to take a minute to review the evidence on my next suspect. First, Dave had a history of poor behavior at Apple Valley. Second, he had a powerful motive to take the cello because he had just found out he wouldn't be allowed in either orchestra next year. Third, Dave possessed a fiery temper, and that temper may have driven him to get even with Mrs. Washington. Fourth, Dave was the Student of the Week in Mrs. O'Connor's class, and when he took the attendance sheet to the office this morning, he would have had access to the display case near the time of the theft.

I also needed to figure out my investigation strategy. At first I wondered whether I should use the door strategy again, but I decided not to push my luck. O

thing I knew for sure was that I didn't want a replay of my first meeting when I angered Brock and put my own safety on the line. I considered myself lucky to escape that meeting unharmed, and I didn't want to take that same risk with the school bully. I needed a completely different approach. I thought for a moment and then came up with an idea that even Jenny would envy.

I knocked on the door and was greeted by one of the most intimidating faces I had ever seen.

It was Brock Fuller.

Instinctively, I jumped back.

"You again!" Brock grumbled. "Dude, what do you want now?"

I gulped and, as calmly as I could, said I needed to ask Mrs. O'Connor a question.

"Why, hello, Chase," said a smiling Mrs. O'Connor when she saw me at the door. She had once taught my sister and was still friendly with my mom. Though the teacher was in the middle of helping Skip with a project, she approached me to see what I wanted.

"It's official school business, Mrs. O'Connor," I truthfully told her. "May I please speak with Dave Morrison outside for a minute?"

"Sure, and say hello to your family for me," she replied.

"I will, Mrs. O'Connor. Thank you."

I then walked with Dave outside into the hall. This time, I was determined to stay on my suspect's good side and keep things positive.

"Yeah, what do you want?" Dave grumbled.

So much for that idea.

"I needed to talk to somebody, and you were the only person I could think of who would understand what I'm going through right now."

"Whoa," Dave said, impressed, "you mean you told my teacher a story just so you could talk to me? I'm surprised at you, man. I didn't think you did stuff like that. I mean, you've always been such a straight arrow, and just a little while ago, even Brock was saying what a dork you were. I'm proud of you, man."

Great. Even if I didn't find the cello today, at least the school bully would be proud of me.

"Well, what I told your teacher was the truth," I said. "But that's not important right now."

"So, what do you want from me?" my new buddy Dave asked.

"I need to talk to you about something that's going on."

"What?"

"You can't play in the orchestra next year, right?" I said. "I just found out there's a chance I can't either, and I'm so mad, I could just . . . I don't know."

I was really happy with how that came out because everything I said was 100 percent true. If the cello wasn't found, I wouldn't be playing in the orchestra—not because of my poor behavior like Dave, but because *nobody* would be playing in it.

"Why can't you play in the orchestra?" Dave asked.

"I don't want to get into that now," I said, trying to change the subject. "Have you ever been so mad that you just wanted to . . . do something?"

"Like what?"

Here's where I had to be careful. I needed to get information from this guy, but I couldn't give out too much of my own. "Like, do something to the cello so nobody would have music."

"Nah."

"Really? Never?" I pushed.

"Well, actually . . . ," Dave said, beginning to loosen up.

"Well, what?"

"Well, actually, earlier this morning when I took the attendance sheet to the office, I saw the cello. I have to admit I did just want to take that thing, run, and go hide it somewhere."

I was getting excited that my "I feel your pain" approach seemed to be working. Dave was in the middle of confessing his crime!

Then, suddenly Dave stopped talking and stood there silently. I still felt I was close to a confession. As great as the joy of finding the cello would be, though, at this moment I was more relieved than anything else, relieved at the thought of not having to investigate the third suspect.

"So, did you?" I said, hardly able to contain my curiosity.

"I couldn't," Dave said.

"Why not?" I asked. This time I was the one beginning to get angry.

"Well," Dave continued, "just as I got close, someone was already there standing right next to the display case, staring at that cello like they were in a trance."

"Who was he?"

"Uh," Dave stumbled, "it wasn't a he; it was a she."

At that moment, I realized two things, neither of them good. First, my hope for a confession from Dave had just disappeared. Second, and even worse, the moment I had feared since my meeting with Mr. Andrews had just arrived.

I knew I would have to investigate the third suspect.

10:11 a.m.

CHAPTER 7

10:12 a.m.

On my way back to class I stopped, knelt down, and put my head in my hands, dreading what was about to happen. I didn't know how to break the news to Jenny. Our friendship was strong, but I didn't know if it was strong enough to handle this.

When I sat down at my desk, Jenny could tell something was wrong. "Any luck with Dave?" she asked softly.

"I thought so at first," I quietly replied. "But then I found out he didn't do it."

"Are you sure?"

"I'm sure."

"So what now?"

"Now we move on to the third suspect."

"Who is it?"

"Well, the third name that Mr. Andrews gave me is actually the same person that Dave Morrison saw by the display case earlier this morning. I'm thinking that person's got to be the thief."

"Chase, tell me already," Jenny insisted. "Who is it?"

"OK. Mr. Andrews thinks the thief could be someone connected to the Spring String Thing, someone who knew the schedule of the day. He thinks the person knew the office would be quiet between 8:55 and 9:15 and took the cello then, before all the parents and other visitors arrived for today's meetings."

Jenny started to laugh. "You mean someone like Amy?" she joked.

I didn't react.

Jenny didn't seem to know if I had heard her. So she repeated herself, this time not in the same joking manner. "I said, Chase, that it sounds like you're talking about Amy."

"That's exactly who I'm talking about."

"Why, you can't possibly think that Amy Simmons took the cello, can you?" Jenny exclaimed.

"Well, that's what Mr. Andrews thinks, and Dave did see her staring at it right before it was taken."

"But why would she take it?" Jenny protested. "What reason would she have for doing something so rotten? I mean, come on, her mom is the one organizing this whole event!"

"That's just it," I responded. "Her mom has been spending lots of time on this event, and you know how Amy feels about that. Come on, you were even standing right outside the office a couple days ago when she and her mom had that big argument. In front of everybody, Amy was yelling about how her mom was spending too much time on the dinner and not enough with her. You also heard her say that she thought her mom cared more about that precious cello than she did about her own daughter. You have to admit, we have to consider Amy our last good suspect."

"I don't have to admit anything!" Jenny argued. "Say what you want, but I know my best friend. There's just no way she did this!"

This is exactly why I was hoping my investigation wouldn't reach this point.

"Come on," I said, trying to calm things down. "I know she's your best friend and you believe in her. But we still need to investigate. If she has the cello, we have to get it back."

"If you want to investigate Amy, go ahead. But you'll have to do it without me!"

Jenny then picked up her papers and moved to an open desk across the room. Recess was only a few minutes away, and I figured I might as well just let her go and cool off. At least I could get some math work done in the meantime. Once we were outside, I would try to find Amy on the playground. There wasn't anything else I could do until then.

Jenny and I had never argued like this before. In fact, as best I can recall, never in her life had she been truly mad at me until a minute ago. As we worked on our math, we stopped every minute or two and looked across the room at each other. I tried to focus on the task at hand, but I kept feeling bad about hurting Jenny. I didn't mean any harm; I was only trying to find the cello and help save the music program.

The next few minutes were extremely quiet. Each time we looked at each other, the tension between us seemed to build. Just as the tension grew to its highest point, the bell rang for recess. The two of us usually played together at recess time.

We would not be playing together today.

10:30 a.m.

CHAPTER 8

10:31 a.m.

Today wasn't going well. Someone had stolen the cello that the school was counting on to raise money at tonight's auction, the thief was at large, Jenny was mad at me, and I still hadn't found any time to practice that tricky cello part before my tryout.

Still, I had to put all this behind me and find a way to talk to Amy Simmons. I could see her walking around the playground at recess, but the problem was that Jenny was with her. I watched them the whole time, just hoping they would separate for some reason so I could talk to Amy alone.

No luck.

But then, two minutes before the bell, Jenny went to the water fountain behind the second-grade rooms to get a drink. I didn't miss a beat. I ran over to Amy as fast as I could.

"Amy, I need to talk to you," I panted.

"What about?"

"I can't tell you now. The bell's going to ring any minute. Meet me by the second-grade water fountain at the beginning of PE."

"Chase, what's going on? It sounds big," Amy said, growing more curious.

"It is. Will you do it?"

"But we might get in trouble."

"Amy, we won't get in trouble. Just ask the coach to use the restroom and then meet me by the water fountain. It'll only take a few minutes."

Amy hesitated. "I'm not sure about this, but you are my friend and I trust you. If you say it's big, then it must be big. OK, Chase, I'll see you at PE."

Just then, the bell rang.

I still didn't want to believe that it was Amy Simmons who stole the cello. In a little while, I would find out for sure.

10:45 a.m.

CHAPTER 9

10:46 a.m.

I was still feeling bad about my argument with Jenny when the class headed back inside from recess. PE was only twenty minutes away and silent reading time awaited. Mrs. Kennedy called it the most valuable part of our day, and I usually loved getting lost in my book. With so much on my mind, I had trouble concentrating today, but I tried to get into the story as best I could.

Even though Jenny knew nothing about my upcoming meeting with Amy, the tension between us seemed to keep building. I guess Jenny couldn't understand how I could possibly suspect her best friend, and I couldn't understand why she was making this personal. I was only trying to find the cello, and that would benefit everybody next year—Jenny, Amy, me, and the rest of the kids in the music program.

Jenny and I did not say one word to each other the whole time, though we did still occasionally make eye contact across the room. The class was completely quiet.

I turned my attention to my meeting with Amy Simmons. She didn't pose a physical threat to me the way that Brock and Dave did, but because of our friendship and because of Jenny, I believed this conversation would be my most difficult of the day.

As I was deciding which investigation strategy to use with Amy, Mrs. Kennedy asked the class to stop reading, put away our books, and line up for PE.

I was only moments away from getting the answers I was seeking.

11:04 a.m.

CHAPTER 10

11:05 a.m.

Coach Turner was waiting for us when we arrived at the kickball diamond, where we always met to begin PE class.

"Listen up!" he yelled. "Mr. Andrews wants us to move PE into the auditorium today. He needs us off the playground. So let's hustle it up, and remember, be quiet walking in the halls!"

That was strange. We never had PE inside except on rainy days, and it was really sunny today. I wondered what was going on.

But I decided not to ask Coach Turner why we were moving inside because in a few minutes I would need to ask to use the restroom. I didn't want to anger him with an unimportant question and run the risk of not being allowed to leave class.

As we walked quietly down the hall to the auditorium, I figured my plan to meet Amy would still work out fine. There was no reason why the change of location had to mean anything.

Once we reached the auditorium, Coach Turner surprised us a second time when he announced he was giving the class a free day. He would pass out all the equipment and we could play any game we wanted.

Now I really wondered what was going on.

Coach Turner never gave free days. He was always saying how important PE was for our health and how he had too much to teach to ever give us a free day. Once some poor girl who was new to the school asked why we never had free days, and Coach Turner exploded. He got right up in her face and screamed, "Do you get free days in math? Free days in science? Free days in spelling? Of course you don't! So don't ask me about free days in physical education!" After that explosion, nobody ever asked again.

After we settled into our various games, a third surprise occurred. Coach Turner put his assistant in charge and left class, something else he never did.

I wasted no time. I ran up to the assistant, jumped up and down as if I were about to have an accident, and asked to use the restroom. The assistant let me go.

I arrived at the water fountain first and waited, figuring that Amy would play for a few minutes before asking to be excused. I thought that was smart of her because if the two of us asked to go at the same time, the assistant might get suspicious.

One minute turned into five, and I was getting nervous, wondering where Amy was. The only person I saw walking in the area was Coach Turner, who was carrying a big box to his car. I didn't think anything of it, though, because I was so worried about Amy.

Finally, a minute later I heard footsteps coming down the hall. "Phew!" I whispered to myself. "It's about time she got here." But as the footsteps grew closer, I realized they were too loud and too heavy to be Amy's. She was little, one of the shortest and lightest kids in the grade. I looked around the corner and saw that it wasn't her.

It was Brock Fuller.

I had to hide—and quick. Brock made it perfectly clear what would happen to me if the two of us ever met again, and I didn't want to take any chances. With nowhere else to go, I ducked down underneath the water fountain and curled myself into the smallest ball I could. I held my breath so Brock wouldn't hear a peep from me. My heart was pounding a mile a minute as Brock bent down and pushed the button on the fountain.

Brock's gulping seemed to last forever, but fortunately, Brock didn't notice me hiding under the fountain. As the sixth grader gulped, I had nothing else to do except stare at Brock's socks. I became almost hypnotized by them. First, I focused on the two blue stripes that wove around the top of each sock. Then, for no reason at all, I began to sniff the socks. Their scent reminded me of the laundry detergent my mom had once used on my clothes. Suddenly, terror struck as I remembered why my mom stopped using that detergent—I was allergic to it.

In fact, my sneezing had gotten so bad that upon discovering my allergy, my mom immediately took all four boxes she had stored in the cabinet above the washing machine and threw them away.

At home, a bunch of sneezes was no big deal. But here, at the feet of Brock Fuller, they could spell disaster. I held my nose and hoped that Brock's gulping was nearing the end. Out of nowhere, however, it came. That same tingle in the nose, followed by those same watery eyes. Before I could stop myself, the rapid-fire sneezing began. "A-choo, a-choo, a-choo!"

Realizing what had just happened, I closed my eyes and curled myself into an even tighter ball, but it was too late. Brock bent down and spotted me.

"Dude, you again! I don't know what you're doing down there, but I've had about enough of you today. Get up!"

I was trying to stand up as quickly as I could, but Brock was in no mood to wait. He grabbed my shirt and helped me the rest of the way up. Brock had me pinned against the wall and looked as if he were about to put me right through it.

Just then, Amy Simmons approached. I noticed her first and then Brock turned to see what I was looking at. As Amy got close to us, all the anger seemed to leave Brock's face. He began to sweat a little bit, and he let go of me. He seemed nervous. It occurred to me what must be going on: Brock had a crush on Amy.

"Hey, Brock, what are you doing?" Amy asked.

"I . . . uh . . . I was just . . . uh," Brock stammered.

"Are you OK, Brock?" Amy said.

"Yeah, Brock, you don't look so good," I added.

"I, uh . . . I . . . uh, I . . ."

"Brock, drink some water. That should make you feel better," Amy suggested.

"No, I . . . I just . . . I just need to get out of here," Brock said as he escaped down the hall.

I let out a sigh of relief.

"Chase, what was that all about?" Amy asked.

"Oh, nothing. Brock and I were just hanging out. You took longer to get here than I thought," I said, changing the subject.

"Well," said Amy, "I'm still not comfortable meeting like this. What's going on?"

I was going to use a new investigation strategy on Amy. I decided against the dork approach because Amy already knew I wasn't a dork. I also didn't think the "I feel your pain" strategy would work as well with Amy as it did with Dave.

Instead, I wanted to try a trick I saw a detective use on television last week—the direct approach. The idea is to come right out and accuse the suspect of the crime and see how the suspect reacts. Usually, according to the detective, suspects are so shocked by this approach that they end up confessing their crimes.

I knew, though, that this strategy came with a certain amount of risk. By accusing Amy of the crime, I would be telling her that the cello had, in fact, been stolen, and Mr. Andrews had asked me not to share this news with anyone.

Still, I figured, things would turn out well either way. If Amy was the thief and she confessed, then this whole nightmare would be over. If she wasn't the thief, then I would explain the whole story to her and trust that she would keep the information to herself.

So without missing a beat, I walked right up to her and said, "Amy, earlier this morning the cello was stolen from the display case, and I think you did it."

Amy was stunned.

"Come on, Amy, it's over. Admit it. Just give the cello back, and I'll go with you to tell your mom and Mr. Andrews that this was all a big misunderstanding."

"What are you talking about?" Amy replied.

"Come on, no more games. Just tell me the truth, and this will all be over."

"Chase, I can't believe you're accusing me of something this bad."

"Amy, enough! I know, OK? I know. I know about the argument with your mom. I know you were staring at the cello earlier this morning. I know you thought your mom cared more about the cello than about you. It all adds up. Just admit it already."

"Chase, this is all a mistake," Amy said, beginning to calm down. "I know I yelled at my mom, but now I realize that the only reason she was spending so much time on tonight's event was because she cared so much about me. She just wanted me, and Jenny, and you, and everybody else to have music next year. I didn't understand that before, but I get it now. And yes, I was staring at the cello earlier. The whole time I was looking at it, I was thinking about how beautiful it was and how I wished someone would buy it tonight to keep our orchestra alive."

At this point, I wasn't sure what to think. I wanted to believe what she was saying, but I still wasn't convinced. I needed more proof before I could let her off the hook once and for all.

"Amy, I hear what you're saying, but I still don't—"

"Listen to me," Amy interrupted. "If all that didn't convince you, think about this. Look at me. See how small I am? Have you seen the cello? It's huge! There's no way I could have lifted that thing out of the display case without making a lot of noise and attracting attention, and I don't know too many kids who could, either. Are you sure a student took the cello? It makes more sense to think that an adult did this."

I never considered the possibility that an adult might have stolen the cello. Before my meeting with Amy, I was hoping that she would be my last suspect because I desperately wanted to bring this investigation to an end.

Now, it seemed that this mystery was only just beginning.

11:27 a.m.

CHAPTER 11

11:28 a.m.

On my way back to the auditorium for the last few minutes of PE, I began to think hard about which adult might actually have had the nerve to steal the cello. It quickly came to me that the only person who seemed to be acting differently today was Coach Turner.

The first thing I remembered was Coach Turner's outburst during morning rehearsal about music being more important at Apple Valley than his sports teams. Second, I recalled my discussion with Brock and his comment that Coach Turner was right about music being a waste of time. Then I thought of the three PE surprises that had never happened before: going inside when it was sunny, having a free day, and the coach leaving his assistant in charge. The final straw was seeing Coach Turner carry a big box to his car while I was waiting for Amy. Could Coach Turner have wanted the yard empty during PE so he could put the cello in his car without anyone noticing?

I needed to talk to somebody. Luckily, just as I was about to enter the auditorium, I saw Mr. Andrews in the hall and asked to speak with him a minute.

"Sure, Chase, come into my office," he replied.

"I need to talk with you, but I don't want to miss anymore class time."

"Don't worry about that. I'll tell Mrs. Kennedy you were with me. Come on in."

We then entered the office, and I sat down in the same chair I sat in earlier.

"Hold on a second, Chase, I'll be right with you," Mr. Andrews said as he walked back into the main office to speak with Mrs. Gonzales.

While I waited, I looked around the principal's office. It was an impressive sight. Medals and trophies filled the tops of his desk and bookcases, and certificates and diplomas hung on every wall. Mr. Andrews seemed to have been awarded every honor possible: Dean's List in college all four years, five-time PTA Honorary Service Award winner, three-time Principal of the Year Award winner, four-time Second Place Finisher in the state music competition, master's degree. The list went on.

I was almost dizzy from reading all the awards when Mr. Andrews returned and took a seat behind his desk.

"So how's your investigation going? Any luck?" he asked.

"Well, Mr. Andrews, I talked to the three people you told me about, and I found out that none of them could possibly have stolen the cello."

"Are you sure about that?" he said with disappointment.

"Yes, sir. I am."

"So, which students do you think we should investigate next?"

"Well, actually, I'm thinking that maybe it wasn't a student after all. The cello is really heavy, and chances are a student wouldn't have been able to lift it out of the display case and carry it away somewhere without being noticed. Maybe we should be looking for an adult."

"Really, you think we should be looking for an adult?"

I had to be careful. I had a strong feeling that Coach Turner was the thief, but I didn't want to say anything yet. I was hoping Mr. Andrews would reach that conclusion on his own.

"Yes, I do," I said.

Just then, Mr. Andrews sat back in his big chair and clasped his hands together behind his head. He looked as if he had something to say to me but wasn't quite sure how to do it.

"Chase," he said, leaning forward, "I have an idea of who might have done it."

"You do?" I had a feeling my principal and I were thinking of the same person.

"Yes," he said. "I'm very impressed with the job you've done today, and I believe I can trust you to handle what I'm about to tell you with maturity and good judgment."

"Yes, sir. Thank you."

"I am very sad to have to say this," Mr. Andrews said softly. "I was really hoping it wouldn't come to this."

"Yes, sir," I said, feeling as if the moment was at hand.

"It hurts me to admit that the thief might be a teacher on my very own staff."

Here it came! He was about to name Coach Turner as the thief.

"Chase, I suspect the thief was . . . no, I really shouldn't be telling you this. I mean, this person and I go way back, and I really shouldn't."

"Please, sir. I can handle the truth." I was practically begging at this point.

Then Mr. Andrews finally came out with it. "OK, I'm afraid the thief may have been Mrs. Washington."

"What? The music teacher?" I responded, completely shocked.

"That's right. I'm afraid Mrs. Washington was the one who took the cello from the display case this morning."

"But why?"

"That's a good question. You see, when you become an adult, there's something called pressure. I'm afraid Mrs. Washington has been under a great deal of pressure lately."

"I'm not sure I understand."

"Well," Mr. Andrews said, "you have to remember that Mrs. Washington has won the state music championship seven times in a row, and this year she's trying to make it eight. Many people think that when you win every year, it gets easier, but it doesn't. The competitions may seem to be all fun and games, but they're not."

"I still don't think I get it."

"Chase, when you win the first year, it's terrific. It's maybe the most exciting thing that you could ever experience. The second year is also wonderful. But every year after that, the pressure grows. Instead of hoping to win, you start expecting to win. Other people start *expecting* you to win. Pretty soon, you feel like you have nothing to gain and everything to lose."

"And you think the pressure made Mrs. Washington steal the cello?"

"Surprisingly, Chase, yes, I do," Mr. Andrews said. "In fact, I was just talking with her a little while ago, and she didn't seem to be herself at all. She was very emotional and she even began raising her voice to me. You know what a sweet lady she is. If she raised her voice to *me*, you know something big has got to be wrong."

"But why would she take the cello?" I asked, still not convinced.

"Think about it this way. If the cello somehow disappeared, then we wouldn't have enough money for any of our orchestras next year, right? And if we didn't have an honors orchestra, then she wouldn't be in the competition and the pressure to keep winning would suddenly go away. She wouldn't have to keep living up to other people's expectations. Life would be much easier for her."

"I still don't know."

"Chase, trust me," Mr. Andrews said sternly. "I know it will be difficult for you, but I'm afraid Mrs. Washington is the next person you need to investigate.

I don't like the idea much myself, but it's something we need to do. Now you hustle along. I'm due to meet with the PTA again in a few minutes."

"OK. I'll go check her out."

"Good boy," Mr. Andrews nodded. "Now you let me know as soon as you come up with something."

I stood up and left the office. I remained unconvinced by my principal's explanation. I would do what he asked me to do and go talk to Mrs. Washington, but I still thought Coach Turner was the more likely suspect.

I was more confused than ever.

11:44 a.m.

CHAPTER 12

11:45 a.m.

The trip from the principal's office to Mrs. Washington's was a short one—too short, in fact, because I wasn't ready to go in yet. I wished I could just keep walking and walking, away from this whole mess, but I knew I had to face up to my challenges, not walk away from them.

Mrs. Washington had the door to her office propped open, probably because of the day's heat. The room wasn't air-conditioned, and I'm guessing she was hoping a nice breeze would flow between her front door and open back window. As I approached the entrance, I heard a loud sobbing noise. Sure enough, when I stuck my head in, I saw Mrs. Washington sitting at her desk, crying.

She saw me standing there and motioned for me to come in. I sat down next to her and noticed that she really did look upset. I didn't want to admit it, but perhaps Mr. Andrews was right about the pressure being too much for her.

"Hi, Chase, what can I do for you?" Mrs. Washington sniffled.

"Are you OK, Mrs. Washington?"

"Oh, that's nice of you to ask," she said, beginning to smile. She had known me since I first started coming to my brother and sister's performances a few years ago. I would always sit up tall in my chair with a pretend cello in one hand and a pretend bow in the other. I would play along with the other kids, and Mrs. Washington would often tell me afterward that she just knew I would one day be a fine musician myself.

"I was walking by and heard you crying. I wanted to see if everything was all right."

"Well," she admitted, "I've actually been under quite a bit of pressure lately."

Oh, no. Could Mr. Andrews have been right about her? I thought.

"Chase," she continued, "music is my life. I love teaching it and I love teaching at this school. All my years teaching kids like your brother and sister have made me incredibly happy. I love this year's orchestras, and I look forward to teaching all the new groups next year. I just don't know what I'll do if we don't raise enough money at the auction tonight."

Mrs. Washington seemed sincere in what she was saying. I was beginning to realize that Mr. Andrews might have been partially correct in what he said about her. Yes, she was under great pressure, but not because she was worried about winning the state championship. She was feeling pressure because she was worried about losing her job and not being able to do what she loved.

I didn't think she stole the cello, but I needed to ask one more question to find out for sure.

"Mrs. Washington, pretty soon the state championship is coming up. Do you get nervous about whether we're going to win or not?"

"Chase, I know many people around here make a big deal about how we do, but quite honestly, winning has never mattered very much to me. I just enjoy having the chance to share our music with new audiences. I really wouldn't be bothered at all if we never won again."

I was fairly good at reading people, and I believed that Mrs. Washington meant what she said. It dawned on me that far from being the thief, Mrs. Washington actually had more at stake—more to lose—than anyone else involved in this whole situation.

"I'm happy to hear you say all this," I said. "I know I've always enjoyed listening to your orchestras. Everybody I know has."

"Well, thank you, and I agree with you. I have always been lucky to be among such supportive people here at Apple Valley. I mean, I can think of only one person who hasn't really been kind to my program, but I try not to pay too much attention to him."

"Oh, who would that be?" I asked, even though I already knew the answer.

"Unfortunately, Coach Turner hasn't been a big fan of mine."

"That's too bad, Mrs. Washington. I've heard stories about some of the things he's said and done because of his jealousy, but I tried not to believe that any of them were true. It's a shame he doesn't feel the way everybody else does about your program."

"Well, I try not to let it bother me. Also, you know what kind of temper he has! So I never thought it would be a good idea to talk to him about it."

At that very moment I stopped and looked out the open front door. I had a feeling someone was standing outside and eavesdropping on our conversation. I wanted to excuse myself and go check it out.

"Mrs. Washington, I've enjoyed talking with you, but I have to head back to class now," I said in a rush.

"OK, Chase, I've enjoyed it too. Keep your fingers crossed about tonight's auction," she said.

"I will. Bye."

As I left, I could see none other than Coach Turner storming away from our area as quickly as he could and heading toward the office. Boy, did he seem mad!

I had the awful feeling that Coach Turner had heard the two of us talking about him and his disrespect for the music program.

Suddenly, two terrible thoughts crept into my mind. First, there was little doubt now that Coach Turner had stolen the cello. Second, and even worse, Coach Turner knew that I was onto him.

"What's Coach Turner going to do," I asked aloud, "now that he knows I'm on his trail?" Instead of worrying about the coach, though, I began to get angry with him. "How dare he steal the cello from the display case!"

Earlier today, I wondered how someone could do this to all the musicians and future musicians at the school. Now I realized that the students were not the only victims of this crime. After talking with Mrs. Washington and hearing about how much she loved teaching music and how music was her life, I knew that she was the biggest victim of all. I felt a strong connection with her and did not want to imagine her looking for another job next year.

I was more determined than ever to investigate Coach Turner and get to the bottom of this mess. Of course, I wanted to find the cello for myself and my classmates, but just as badly, I wanted to find it for the music teacher whom I now admired more than ever before. This investigation was not just about music anymore.

Now it was personal.

12:02 p.m.

CHAPTER 13

12:03 p.m.

I approached my classroom door only a few minutes before lunch started. The first thing I wanted to do was find Jenny and put an end to the tension between us. I now knew that Amy didn't steal the cello, and I needed to tell Jenny that. Once she knew that I no longer considered Amy a suspect and was instead focusing on Coach Turner, we could get back together and try to figure out a way to catch the real thief and track down the cello.

I was also thinking ahead. Already, I had worked out my entire lunch schedule. First I would go talk to Mr. Andrews and tell him that it was Coach Turner who stole the cello, not Mrs. Washington. Next I would investigate the coach and find out where the cello was hidden. Then, if there was any time left, I would try to prepare for my tryout by practicing that tricky cello part.

Because today was the last day before spring break, the lunch period was going to be longer than normal: a full hour instead of the usual forty-five minutes. This was great news because I would have plenty of time to accomplish everything I wanted. I would also be more relaxed investigating during lunch because I knew I wouldn't be missing anything in class during that time.

I walked into the room, sat down at my desk, and looked over at Jenny. Everybody was in the middle of cleaning up and getting ready for lunch. Mrs. Kennedy didn't even ask me where I'd been all this time. I guess Mr. Andrews had called earlier, as he said he would, to tell her that I was with him.

Just as I was about to whisper something to Jenny, the intercom signal went off, indicating that an announcement from the office was on its way.

"Boys and girls, this is Principal Andrews, and this is the moment you have all been waiting for," the message began. "I would like to take a moment to announce the winner of the 'Win Lunch with the Mystery Teacher' raffle and reveal the identity of the mystery teacher."

With so much on my mind, I had completely forgotten about the raffle. On a regular day I would have been very interested in hearing these names, but today it didn't seem quite so important. Still, I sat quietly and listened to Mr. Andrews. All the other kids in the class had been looking forward to the announcement all day and couldn't wait to hear it. They had been talking about it for weeks, ever since the principal and the PTA announced that because tonight's dinner and auction were for adults only, they wanted to do something special for the students. Everyone wanted to win badly. And if they didn't, they were at least hoping the winner was someone in the class or someone else at school they knew.

Mr. Andrews continued, "Before naming the winner, though, I need to tell you of a change that we are making in the contest. Originally, the winner was going to have lunch with the mystery teacher sometime after spring break. Now, I am happy to report that the winner will have lunch with the mystery teacher *today*."

The excitement intensified when my classmates heard that. Now they all wanted to win the raffle even more.

Finally, Mr. Andrews was ready to announce the winner. "Boys and girls, it is my pleasure to announce that the winner of the first annual 'Win Lunch with the Mystery Teacher' raffle is Chase Manning."

My classmates started to make so much noise cheering for me that they almost forgot to listen to part two of the announcement. As soon as they heard Mr. Andrews begin to speak again, though, they all got quiet.

"And," he continued, "this year's mystery teacher is Coach Bill Turner."

12:09 p.m.

CHAPTER 14

12:10 p.m.

The absolute last thing I wanted right now was to go out to lunch with Coach Turner. While almost every other kid in school would have traded places with me in a heartbeat, winning the raffle represented the worst possible luck at the worst possible time.

Now all of my lunch plans would have to be put on hold. Because I would be off campus, I wouldn't be able to fix things with Jenny, I wouldn't be able to tell Mr. Andrews everything I had learned about Coach Turner, and there was no way I'd have time to practice for my tryout.

Interestingly enough, the one thing I could do was investigate Coach Turner. In fact, it was very possible the missing cello was in the trunk of the car that the two of us would be taking to lunch. That was the only good news; I would be able to check out the car and have plenty of time to talk to Coach Turner.

More than anything else, though, I was scared. Coach Turner had a terrible temper and in all likelihood knew that I was onto him. When I thought of investigating the coach, I had always assumed it would be at school, where I would be safe and have plenty of people around me if things got difficult.

Now we would be alone. As the driver, Coach Turner would be in charge of deciding where we were going, and I would have nowhere to turn for help. Even worse, whatever the coach planned to do, he'd have more time than usual to do it because of today's extended lunch period.

All these thoughts were racing through my mind while Mrs. Kennedy practically grabbed me by the hand the moment my name was announced and dragged me down the hall to the office where I would meet the coach.

I wasn't normally one to make excuses, but I decided I was going to do everything I could to get out of going to lunch today.

"Mrs. Kennedy, wait!" I said as she hustled me to the office.

"What is it, Chase?" she asked, stopping outside the door to see what I wanted. "You don't sound as excited as I thought you'd be."

"It's not that," I replied, searching for something to say. "But don't I need a permission slip to leave school? Remember, that's what you said when Bobby couldn't go on that field trip last month." I was proud of that quick thought and hoped it would work.

"Don't worry, Mr. Andrews called your mom and got her permission before he made his announcement."

I then tried another excuse. "Mrs. Kennedy, can't I go after spring break? I was really hoping I could practice for my orchestra tryout during lunch."

"Oh, you'll find some time later this afternoon for that. Relax. You won. Go enjoy yourself," she suggested.

"You're right, it's just that . . . I brought this really great lunch to school today, and I've been looking forward to eating it all day."

"You'll eat it when you get home. Go on."

"Are you sure?"

"Chase, of course I'm sure. Do you know how many kids would love to be in your shoes right now?"

That gave me an idea.

"You know, Mrs. Kennedy, I've been thinking. I've got two good buddies in Mrs. O'Connor's class. Maybe you know them, Brock Fuller and Dave Morrison. I think I'd like to let one of them go in my place."

"That's a nice offer, dear. Really, it is, but that's out

of the question. You won, you'll go. I'll hear no more about it. You don't want to be disrespectful to Coach Turner, do you?"

I had to bite down hard on my lip not to laugh at that one. *Me* be disrespectful to the *coach*? That was a good one.

I realized that I was out of excuses and Mrs. Kennedy was out of patience. I wanted to let her in on the whole story right then and there, but I couldn't because as we entered the office, Coach Turner and Mr. Andrews were waiting for us, along with Mrs. Simmons and a photographer.

"Congratulations, Chase!" Mr. Andrews called out.

"Yes, indeed," agreed Mrs. Simmons.

Coach Turner didn't say a word.

"I'm so happy," Mrs. Simmons continued, "that such a nice young man won the raffle. You know, my daughter, Amy, is always saying such wonderful things about you, Chase. She just thinks the world of you."

If Mrs. Simmons knew I accused her daughter of being a thief this morning, she might not be so happy for me.

"Come on, gather around, everybody," Mr. Andrews said. "Let's get a picture of this special moment for the school yearbook. Mrs. Simmons and Mrs. Kennedy, why don't you two stand in the middle. I'll stand on the right, and Chase and Coach Turner can stand together on the left."

I had a creepy feeling standing next to Coach Turner for the picture. And this was in the office with other people around. I didn't want to think about what it would be like once the two of us were alone.

The photographer asked everyone to smile big for the camera, but that was too much to ask right now. I knew my family and friends would see this picture in the yearbook, so I managed a half smile but nothing more.

When all the pictures and congratulations were over, Coach Turner motioned for me to follow him out to his car in the teachers' parking lot.

I was silent as I made my way outside. I didn't know where I was headed, what was going to happen, or when I would be back.

One thing I did know. I sure wasn't looking forward to getting in that car.

12:21 p.m.

CHAPTER 15

12:22 p.m.

As Coach pulled out of the parking lot, I decided that this couldn't be a coincidence. What were the odds that out of 620 students at Apple Valley, my raffle ticket would be the one picked, while at the same time, out of thirty faculty members, Coach Turner would be the mystery teacher?

Something was up, and I thought I knew what it was. I believed that Coach Turner overheard my conversation with Mrs. Washington and then stormed to the office just before the raffle was about to occur. Then he went to Mr. Andrews, demanded to be the mystery teacher, and fixed it so that I won. After that, he came up with the idea of moving lunch to today, rather than after spring break, so he could take me off campus and scare me enough to end the investigation.

If that had been Coach Turner's plan, I had to admit it was working so far. I was scared. To make things worse,

I didn't know if we were really even going to lunch. Maybe the coach was going to take me somewhere until 3:00 p.m. so that when we got back to school, it would be too late to do anything about the cello. I also thought of other things Coach Turner could have in store for me, but then I decided I had better start thinking about something else.

My mind wandered. First I thought about the cello part I still needed to practice. Next, patching things up with Jenny entered my mind. Just then, Coach Turner drove over a bump and something made a thud in the trunk. Suddenly I remembered that big box Coach Turner carried to his car during PE. That thud very well could have been the cello. Hopefully, no harm had just come to it.

Ten minutes into the ride and still not a word was exchanged between the two of us. I stared out the window and realized we were heading down a road I had never been on before. Apple Valley wasn't that large of a place. I had lived here all my life and there wasn't much I hadn't seen. Where exactly were we going?

Suddenly, Coach Turner stopped the car. I wasn't sure why. We were nowhere near any restaurants, and the car seemed to be working fine. Without explanation, Coach undid his seatbelt, got out, and shut the door behind him. As he stood next to the driver's side door, he pulled a cell phone from his pocket and began talking. He was annoyed. I couldn't tell whether he was making or answering a call. Through the door I was able to hear only bits and pieces of the conversation.

"Yeah, I got it . . . Don't worry, I'll be out of there right after school . . . I told you not to worry . . . I said I'd take care of everything, and I did . . . I gotta go. No, I can't talk now. I gotta go."

With that, he hung up the phone, got back in the car, and started driving again. A million questions raced through my mind, but at this moment my fear prevented me from asking any of them.

A few minutes later, the coach seemed to settle down, but that calmness would prove to be only temporary.

Anger returned soon after when he looked in the rearview mirror and noticed a police car following behind us. The siren was blaring, and the officer was motioning for the coach to pull over to the side of the road.

"What in the world is going on?" Coach Turner grumbled to himself. "I'm not speeding. I'm not driving recklessly. Why is this guy pulling me over?"

I didn't know why we were being pulled over, either. Maybe the police had somehow found out about the stolen cello and followed Coach Turner in order to arrest him.

Both cars pulled over to the side of the road and the officer approached Coach Turner's window.

"Good afternoon, sir," the officer said, "could you please open your trunk?"

I couldn't believe my luck. I had him now!

"What's this all about, Officer?" Coach Turner replied, trying to hold his temper.

"Sir, you're about to enter a protected environmental area. It's our policy this time of year to check the trunks of all cars driving up this road to make sure that no dangerous materials enter the area."

"Oh," I mumbled to myself, turning my body away from the adults' conversation. "I didn't expect that. But still, we're going to get to see inside the trunk."

"Officer, is this really necessary?" Coach asked, growing impatient.

"Yes, sir, it is."

"But, Officer, my name is Bill Turner. I am the PE coach at Apple Valley Elementary. My football teams have won five league championships. Maybe you've heard of me?"

"No, I'm afraid I haven't," the officer said.

"Oh," said the coach, his feelings slightly hurt.

"Anyway, I am taking my student Chase to lunch today, and our schedule is very tight. I need to get him back to school right after we eat. Can't have the young lad missing out on any learning, can we?"

"No, Coach, we can't. But it will only take me a few moments to inspect the trunk."

"Officer, I know you're just doing your job. But we're only going to grab a quick lunch and head back to school. We're not going to damage the environment, and besides, there's nothing interesting in the trunk. I promise you. Could you please just let us go?"

As the officer paused to make a decision, I wanted to tell him that there was probably something very interesting in the trunk, but I was too scared to say anything. Instead, I was hoping the officer wouldn't fall for Coach's story.

"Well, we can't have the boy be late getting back to school," said the officer. "OK, go ahead. Have a nice lunch."

Coach Turner was openly thrilled; I was silently furious.

"Oh, thank you, Officer," Coach beamed. "All of us at Apple Valley Elementary appreciate this very much."

With that, the officer returned to his car, Coach Turner started the engine, and the two of us continued the drive to lunch.

"We'll be there in just a minute," Coach said, finally breaking his silence with me.

"Where are we going, Coach?" I asked, though I wasn't sure if I actually wanted to know the answer. We really were driving in the middle of nowhere.

"There's a place I know that cooks the best burgers in town," Coach said. "Not too many people know about it. I thought it would be a nice spot for lunch."

Boy, was I relieved to hear that. We actually were going to lunch. Coach then pulled into a dirt parking lot, stopped the car, and rubbed his stomach, as if he'd been looking forward to this burger all day.

As I headed to the restaurant, Coach yelled, "Hold on a minute, Chase. I have to check something in my trunk."

12:34 p.m.

CHAPTER 16

12:35 p.m.

The mere mention of the word "trunk" made me freeze instantly. I then walked back to the car, wondering why the coach wasn't being more discrete. *This is strange,* I thought to myself, *I would've thought that Coach Turner would want to keep me away from the trunk. Why would he open it right here in front of me when he's got the cello in there?*

Coach Turner opened the trunk, reached down, and grabbed what he was looking for.

"There it is!" he called out.

I covered my eyes with my hands, not wanting to see what the coach had grabbed.

"There's my wallet! I thought I'd lost that thing!" Coach exclaimed.

I looked. Sure enough, Coach Turner was holding his wallet. But that's not all he had in that trunk.

He had practically every piece of camping gear ever invented.

Coach Turner spent the next few minutes describing—in way too much detail—all the camping equipment he owned. He then explained that after school he and his wife were headed to the mountains for a week of camping with their two kids.

"That's why I had to give you kids a free day earlier and put my assistant in charge," he said. "I hated to do it, but we still had a lot of details to take care of for our trip. I knew I wouldn't have any time after school to do it because we have to leave right at three in order to arrive before dark. So I had to do everything during class. I had to call my wife a couple of times and move some boxes of sleeping bags from my office to my car."

I realized that some of my best evidence against the coach was disappearing. Still, I remembered his comments during the rehearsal, his storming to the office before lunch, and his overall disrespect for the music program. I wasn't ready to let him off the hook just yet.

The two of us sat at the counter on the right side of the restaurant and were served quickly. The burgers were great, and we attacked our food with the ferocity of lions.

"I couldn't wait a minute longer to get my hands on this burger!" the coach said in between bites. "That's why I didn't want to stop and have the trunk inspected. I was starved."

Coach Turner finished first and started telling me about all the times he'd been camping before.

I was no longer scared; I was bored. Coach went on and on with his camping stories, and after a while, I just stopped listening. Coach Turner didn't even realize that I had stopped listening. He continued to go on with his stories.

Fortunately, in the background there was some nice music playing. So I just listened to that and began to relax.

"You know," Coach said, taking a break from his camping stories, "this really is beautiful music. Not too many people know this, but I love music—especially the kind our orchestras play at school."

I wasn't sure whether I was hearing correctly.

"I know I criticize our music program," the coach said, "and I know I give Mrs. Washington a hard time every now and then. I have to admit, though, she does great work. I still think she gets too much attention from everybody, but she does do great work."

Now I didn't know what to think. Luckily for me,

Coach Turner went back to his camping stories, giving me plenty of time to sort through my thoughts.

The rest of the evidence against the coach seemed to be disappearing as well. If, deep down inside, he really did respect Mrs. Washington, then his motive for stealing the cello—jealousy—might not fit anymore. Also, my fears were turning out to be only in my head. After all, the coach did take me to lunch, display his trunk openly, and explain away most of my concerns.

I was now back at square one. Who could have done this? And where could that cello be?

Out of the blue, another adult suspect popped into my mind. "No, it couldn't be him," I said to myself after considering the idea for a moment. I went back to my burger and kept thinking.

A moment later, Coach Turner switched from camping stories to coaching stories. Even though they were just as boring, at least they were a new kind of boring.

"I remember three years ago, our football team made it to the championship game. It was my best team ever, but we lost. I tell you, there's something about coming in second place that does strange things to a man. I mean, it's heartbreaking. To come so close and not win, it'll drive you bananas. Chase, never underestimate what second place can do to you."

As Coach Turner continued his story, I kept repeating certain words over and over again to myself: "second place . . . drive you bananas . . . second place . . . bananas . . . heartbreaking . . . second place . . . does strange things to a man."

And then it hit me!

Mr. Andrews was a music teacher before he became a principal. He competed in the state championship four times against Mrs. Washington and came in second every time. The walls in his office were filled with second place plaques—no first place ones. If Coach Turner was right about second place driving a man bananas and making him do strange things, then what could finishing in second place *four times* do to someone?

Could it lead him to steal a cello in order to put the woman who beat him out of work?

I didn't know. As Coach Turner kept going with his sports stories, I thought some more about the day and about how Mr. Andrews was connected to everything. Immediately, I remembered the start of PE class when Coach Turner sent the kids to the auditorium because Mr. Andrews said he needed the playground clear.

Maybe it was Mr. Andrews who needed the playground free so he could hide the cello somewhere! Possibly, but I didn't want to get ahead of myself.

Then, all of a sudden, a question popped into my mind. "Coach, I'm sorry to interrupt your story, but let me ask you something."

"What is it, Chase?"

"How'd you get to be the mystery teacher today?"

"I don't know. I was as surprised as anybody. Mr. Andrews told all the teachers we would pick somebody after vacation, but just before lunch he called me to his office. I was very upset, too, because he called me during class, and I hate being interrupted in the middle of class. So I stormed down the hall, passed Mrs. Washington's office, and asked the principal what he wanted."

So that's why Coach was so angry before. He didn't overhear my conversation with the music teacher. He was mad about being interrupted during class. The pieces were beginning to fit together!

"So," Coach went on, "when I walked into Mr. Andrews's office, he said he needed me to take you to lunch today."

"You mean, he asked you to take the *raffle winner* to lunch, don't you?" I asked.

"Raffle?" Coach asked, confused. "There was no raffle. He just asked me to take you to lunch and to take my time about it. He even said it was OK if I kept you out past the bell."

"You mean there was no raffle?" I asked, still not believing what I was hearing. "No tickets or drawing or anything like that?"

"Nope. There was nothing like that," the coach assured me.

"And he asked you to take me, by name?"

"Yep, he said to take Chase Manning out to lunch today."

That sealed it. I now knew beyond a shadow of a doubt that Mr. Andrews must have stolen the cello. Earlier, I thought that the coach took me to lunch to ruin my investigation. But it was really the principal who asked the coach to take me to lunch to ruin the investigation. Come to think of it, that had to be why Mr. Andrews had me investigate Brock, Dave, Amy, and Mrs. Washington.

It was all a lie! Mr. Andrews was just trying to throw me off the real trail and buy time until three o'clock, when he could escape unnoticed for two whole weeks.

As I was figuring all this out, Coach Turner went to pay the bill. We then headed back to school. My feelings about the coach were now far more positive than they were on the way to the restaurant. There was a bit of a friendship between us now, and I had to admit, the burger *was* the best in town.

We entered the teachers' parking lot a few minutes before the end of lunch. I got out of the car and looked at everybody on the playground.

I couldn't believe what I saw.

1:07 p.m.

CHAPTER 17

1:08 p.m.

Because of today's extended lunch period and because spring break was less than two hours away, I expected all the kids to be on the playground having the recess of their lives. They weren't.

At first, it appeared that some sort of accident must have occurred while the coach and I were gone. Students were huddled together in small groups; many kids were crying. The school counselor, psychologist, nurse, and even some teachers were out on the playground trying to console the most emotional ones and keep them calm. Few kids were playing.

The school seemed to be in a state of shock.

Then I realized what must have happened. They knew. Sometime during lunch, everybody must have found out about the missing cello. The secret that I had tried so hard to protect had been revealed.

I started thinking about who might have let the cat out of the bag. Was it done by accident or on purpose? Was it Jenny, who was still mad about our argument? Was it Amy, who was angry that I accused her of stealing the cello? Or could it have been Mr. Andrews, who, sensing that I was closing in on him, leaked the information in order to cause chaos and make my job that much more difficult? Maybe the principal would blame me for spilling the beans.

I then began to wonder why nobody seemed to be looking for the cello. Maybe they were still in shock, or maybe they thought the thief and cello were both long gone and that searching for them would be a waste of time. But the others didn't know what I knew—that if the principal did do it, the cello would still be on campus somewhere because he hadn't left school all day.

At 1:10 p.m., the bell rang to bring this long, difficult lunch period to an end. I usually hustled to class right at the sound of the bell, but today I just stood there on the playground, lost in my thoughts. In a minute I was the only person left out there. I needed some time to figure out my next move.

I was completely convinced that Mr. Andrews was the culprit. It sounded crazy, but the evidence did add up. Investigating the principal *was* going to be trickier now that the whole school knew about the theft. At this stage, however, there was no turning back.

It promised to be an interesting afternoon.

1:13 p.m.

CHAPTER 18

1:14 p.m.

I entered the room just as my classmates were settling into what was usually our favorite part of the week—choice time, when we could do any activity we wished. Normally, I would have been playing chess with Jenny, using the computer, or building a model on the rug with my other friends. Today, I wasn't in the mood for any games.

The rest of the class didn't look much happier and didn't appear to be in the mood for their usual activities, either. Most of the kids had chosen to read or draw quietly.

Mrs. Kennedy saw the look on my face, and I think she could tell I had heard the bad news. She called me over to her desk and asked how my lunch with Coach Turner went. After I told her it was fine, she suggested that I still use this time to practice for this afternoon's tryout because you never know, the cello might turn up later in the day.

I wasn't feeling quite as optimistic, but I still went to the closet to grab my instrument. On my way I saw Jenny, who was drawing, and took a seat next to her. She was as sad as I had ever seen her. It wasn't hard to figure out why. The two of us had argued earlier, I had accused her best friend of stealing the cello, and now I noticed she had a big bandage on her elbow.

"What happened to your arm?"

"I fell during PE and had to go to the nurse," Jenny replied.

"Does it hurt?"

"It's not too bad, compared to everything else that's happened today."

I figured this was as good a time as any to clear the air with her. "Listen, Jenny, I'm sorry about everything with Amy. I talked to her, and I found out that she didn't do it."

"I know. I feel bad, too. I understand you were just trying to get the cello back."

"Thanks," I said, beginning to feel a whole lot better about everything.

"I also know that what you did wasn't easy. It takes courage to investigate a friend. That must have been hard for you."

We then smiled at each other and put an end to the tension between us. Our conversation shifted to the investigation.

"I have to figure out my next move," I said.

"What for? That cello's got to be a hundred miles from here by now."

"No, Jenny," I replied sharply, "it's still here at school somewhere. I know it is."

"How do you know?"

I whispered to her as softly as I could, "I know who did it! It wasn't Brock or Dave or Amy or any other student."

"Tell me then, Chase! Who was it?"

"It was Mr. Andrews."

"What? The principal?" she blurted.

"Shh!" I commanded.

Mrs. Kennedy looked over at us and cleared her throat.

"Sorry," she whispered, "but I wasn't expecting anything like that. Are you sure it was Mr. Andrews?"

"Yes, I know it's him, and he hasn't left school all day because of his meetings with the PTA about tonight. So the cello must be here somewhere."

"Chase, do you have proof? I mean, you better have

proof if you're going to accuse the principal," she warned.

I went on to share with Jenny all the evidence I had gathered on Mr. Andrews, especially the part about the phony raffle.

Jenny believed me and then, much to my surprise, revealed even more evidence against the principal. "Chase, when I was walking to the nurse's office during PE, I overheard Mr. Andrews and Mrs. Washington talking."

"Yeah, I know about that. Mr. Andrews told me he had spoken with her and that she was getting really emotional. He thought she was cracking under the pressure and—"

"No, Chase, that's not what happened at all," she interrupted. "He was the one getting emotional. He was getting all worked up and yelling at her, saying things like, 'Good luck finding a new job next year' and 'I knew I'd finally beat you sooner or later.' I didn't understand what he meant by all that, but now it makes sense."

"So that's why she was crying like that when I went in to talk to her."

"Chase, I'm convinced the principal did it, but if we're going to accuse him, we need even more proof, like a witness!"

"You're right, but what kind of evidence can we get?"

The two of us paused for a moment. Then suddenly it hit me!

"I know!" I declared. "The security camera! If Mr. Andrews took the cello, then there must be a tape of it in the security room."

Two years ago, a series of thefts occurred at Apple Valley, and the school installed security cameras for protection. I hadn't thought much about them before today, but I knew there was one camera directly facing the entryway to the office. If Mr. Andrews had stolen the cello, the camera definitely would have caught it on tape.

"Oh, that's great!" Jenny cheered. "You have to go tell Mrs. Kennedy right now! She'll want to help us."

Slowly, I walked up to Mrs. Kennedy. It wasn't every day that you accused your teacher's boss of the biggest crime in school history, and I was nervous about how she would react.

"Mrs. Kennedy," I began, "I have some things to tell you. They may sound crazy, they may be hard to believe, but I promise you that they're all true."

Pulling a chair beside her, she said, "Sit down. Tell me what's going on."

I went on to explain everything to her. I told her about my discovery of the missing cello earlier that morning, my conversations with Mr. Andrews, my investigation of the three kids, my talk with Mrs. Washington, my lunch with Coach Turner, and, finally, my reasons for suspecting the principal. I then asked for her permission to go find Kenny, the custodian, so I could open up the security room and find the tape from this morning.

"I'm stunned," she replied, clutching the handle of her chair and bracing herself.

Uh-oh, what did I just do?

Then, after taking a minute to think things through, a change came over her. My teacher didn't seem shocked anymore. She didn't seem mad. She seemed completely calm.

"Mrs. Kennedy, is everything OK?" I asked, hoping I didn't just blow my whole investigation.

"Chase," she said, smiling, "what you're saying absolutely sounds crazy, but do you know what? I trust you, and I believe what you're telling me. Your excuses right before lunch and your being late a few times today suddenly make more sense to me, as well."

Wow, was I relieved to hear that.

"Chase," she implored, "you have permission to do whatever you need to do. Time's running out, and you need to find that cello."

I thanked her. Then I hesitated.

"Is something wrong?" she asked.

"I'm worried about my tryout today. Earlier this morning Mrs. Washington told me to practice this cello part I'm having trouble with, and I haven't had time to do it yet. I know I need to find Kenny as soon as possible, but I wish I had time to practice first."

"Chase, listen to me. I know you're concerned about making next year's honors orchestra, but you need to keep your eye on the ball. If you don't find that cello, it won't matter how well your tryout goes because there won't *be* an honors orchestra next year. You have worked hard on your music, and you have to trust that all your practice will pay off this afternoon."

I knew she was right. I appreciated her confidence in me, and for the first time in a while, I felt energetic and optimistic.

"OK, Mrs. Kennedy, I'll go now."

"Go get 'em."

I was so excited, I reached out and gave her a nice fist bump before racing off to find Kenny. Some of the kids started laughing at my fist bump, but I was so focused on my mission, I didn't care. I was closing in now.

I had a thief to catch.

1:41 p.m.

CHAPTER 19

1:42 p.m.

Three questions ran through my mind on my way out the door. First, where could Kenny be right now? Second, would the custodian be willing to open the door to the security room for me? And third, did I just fist-bump Mrs. Kennedy?

The last question I could answer. Yes, I had, in fact, just fist-bumped my teacher. No big deal.

I needed to find the answer to my first question. I decided to start looking for Kenny on the far side of the school and then work my way down toward the office and auditorium. I saw Kenny all the time around campus and figured that tracking him down would be a piece of cake.

Kenny was nowhere to be found on the playground, by the library, or in the computer lab. I checked the hallways by the third- and second-grade rooms next, and still no sign of Kenny. After that came the first-grade and kindergarten areas.

No luck.

I was beginning to get worried. Could something have happened to Kenny? I continued looking near the office and auditorium.

Still no luck.

There was only one more place I could think of to check—the cafeteria. "Well," I said to myself, "lunch did just end a little while ago. Maybe Kenny's in there cleaning."

I headed straight for the cafeteria and was nearly knocked backward by what I heard.

Kenny's radio was so loud, I felt as if I were at a rock concert. I peeked inside, and sure enough, Kenny was in there mopping the floor and dancing to the beat of the music.

Kenny was a cool guy. All the kids liked him because he smiled and greeted us by name every morning. Also, he had the biggest muscles any of us had ever seen. He used to be a bodybuilder when he was younger.

I thought about walking across the room to talk to Kenny, but I didn't want my footprints to mess up the mopping. So I decided to call out the custodian's name and hope that Kenny could hear me over the music.

"Kenny!" I yelled across the cafeteria.

No answer. Just more dancing and mopping.

I tried again. "Hey, Kenny!" I screamed at the top of my lungs.

The custodian still couldn't hear me.

This approach wasn't going to work. I had to figure out another way to get Kenny's attention. I then saw the light switch just inside the door.

Should I?

I decided to go for it and turned off the lights to the cafeteria.

Kenny freaked out when the room went dark all of a sudden. He stopped dancing, turned off his music, and looked over at the door.

"Chase, is that you?" Kenny asked. His older son, Ricky, also went to Apple Valley. He and I were once classmates, and we remained friends.

"Yes, Kenny, it's me. I'm sorry about the lights. I tried calling your name, but the music was too loud for you to hear me."

"Don't worry about it," he said, smiling. "What can I do for you?"

I had to choose my words carefully. No student had ever been in the security room before, and I didn't know if Kenny would let me be the first. But today was full of firsts, and I wanted the streak to continue. I decided to play it cool.

"Kenny, Mrs. Kennedy wanted me to check on something in the security room for a minute. Would you mind opening the door for me, please?"

"I'm really not supposed to, Chase. Is it important?"

"Oh, yes, it is. You have no idea how important."

Kenny just stood there looking into my eyes, and I think he could tell how sincere I was in what I was saying. "I probably shouldn't let you in there," the custodian said, pausing, "but I will."

"Oh, thank you. I really appreciate it." I was thrilled that Kenny agreed to do this for me.

The two of us then walked down the hall, turned left, and passed the office. I was incredibly relieved to be only a few seconds away from getting into the security room and finding the tape that would prove once and for all that Mr. Andrews had stolen the cello.

At the door of the security room, Kenny pulled a key chain out of his pocket and found the right key. He was just about to unlock the door when we heard footsteps coming down the hall.

Just then, Mr. Andrews turned the corner and saw what was happening. The principal gave me a fierce look.

This was our third meeting of the day. It was the first time, however, that I saw Mr. Andrews not as my principal and supporter, but as the thief who'd been sending me on a wild goose chase all day. And it was the first time that Mr. Andrews saw me not just as some kid whom he could easily manipulate, but as the person who could identify him as the thief.

Very calmly, Mr. Andrews turned his attention to the custodian. "Kenny, the PTA and I need you in the faculty lounge right now."

"Yes, sir. Right away," Kenny replied.

Then the principal looked back at me, the kid who just a moment ago had come so close to finding the evidence I was seeking. "Chase, you go ahead back to class."

"Yes, Mr. Andrews," I said, disappointed.

I had been denied.

1:53 p.m.

CHAPTER 20

1:54 p.m.

My emotions had been going up and down like a roller coaster all day. Five minutes ago, I was all set to capture the final piece of the puzzle and get the proof I needed to implicate Mr. Andrews. Now I was frustrated.

I walked back into class and sat down next to Mrs. Kennedy. Jenny came right over. I guess they could tell that things hadn't gone as planned. I told them everything that had happened. I told them how close I had come.

"Let's think. What else can we try?" said Jenny, checking her watch.

I was still lost in my own thoughts. "I was so close," I said to myself, shaking my head. "So close."

"Come on, Chase," Mrs. Kennedy said. "Jenny's right. We have to forget about the past and figure out our next move."

"That key," I said, still shaking my head, "that key was practically inside the knob."

"Chase, come on, snap out of it," Mrs. Kennedy urged.

"The key!" Jenny repeated. "That's it!"

"Jenny's right," I said, suddenly coming out of my daze. "Mr. Andrews took Kenny away from me, but we don't need Kenny to enter the security room. We just need a key."

"Yeah," Jenny said, "we have to find another key!"

"Mrs. Kennedy," I asked, "do you have a key to the security room?"

"No, I'm afraid I don't."

Jenny and I dropped our heads in disappointment upon hearing her answer.

"Oh, wait! I have a master key. It opens every lock in the school," Mrs. Kennedy remembered.

"All right!" Jenny and I said together.

"Except—"

"Except what, Mrs. Kennedy?" we asked, our heads falling back down in disappointment.

"The only thing, kids," she explained, "is that the security room was built after I received my master key. I'm not sure if it will work in the lock. I've never tried it."

"We have to see, though," Jenny insisted, checking her watch once again.

"It's worth a shot," I said in agreement.

"Jenny, you go with him this time. It will help him to have some backup."

"Good idea, Mrs. Kennedy," I replied, thinking it would be nice to have someone I could trust by my side.

All of a sudden a pained expression appeared on Jenny's face.

"Gee, I'd like to help, but I'm afraid I can't," she said.

"What do you mean, you *can't*?" I asked.

"My tryout starts in a minute, and I have to get to the auditorium."

"Seriously, Jenny, you're leaving me *now*?"

"I have to. You know how important this tryout is to me and my family."

"It's important to me, too, but if we don't find the cello, there will be nothing to try out *for*. What good is it to make the honors orchestra when it might not exist next year?" I couldn't believe this.

"I'm sorry, but I have to go."

"But, Jenny, wait—"

It was too late. She was already halfway out the door before I could complete my sentence.

Mrs. Kennedy could tell how disappointed I was, but she still reached out and handed me the key. "Chase, go back to that security room and finish what you started. I know you wanted Jenny to go with you, but there's no time to waste. You give that key a try this instant."

Mrs. Kennedy was right.

I grabbed the key and bolted down to the security room. Though I was upset that Jenny had chosen to go to her tryout instead of helping me, I was also relieved that this time around I could head straight for the door and not have to spend any time finding the custodian and asking for his key. A couple questions, however, did still remain. Would the key work? And would I be able to enter the security room without being noticed by Mr. Andrews?

Time was running out. This looked like my last chance to catch the thief.

2:02 p.m.

CHAPTER 21

2:03 p.m.

I traveled back down to the security room like an officer in a police movie who enters a suspect's apartment, hides with his back to the wall, and looks in every direction before taking a step forward. I knew if Mr. Andrews spotted me again, my investigation would be all over. Having Jenny around as an extra pair of eyes sure would have helped right now, but I couldn't afford to let myself be distracted. So I took my time and was as careful as possible.

After a few moments, I was ready to turn the final corner and walk the last twenty yards to the security room. Nobody had noticed me yet, and the coast was clear. I looked around one last time. Still nobody. I could now see the security room door.

I made a run for it.

"That's strange," I said to myself after making it there easily. "Mr. Andrews saw me here a little while ago. He knows I'm onto him, yet he left the hallway unguarded.

At the very least, I figured he'd have someone in the area keeping an eye out for me."

But there was not a soul out there.

I was now ready to try the master key. "I sure hope this works," I whispered. My heart was racing a mile a minute as I put the key in the door. It fit! But would it open the door?

I looked around one last time and turned the knob.

It worked!

My heart was pounding even louder now. I gently pushed open the door and stepped inside. As I walked into the security room, I grabbed the knob on the other side of the door with both hands and didn't take my eyes off it until I had guided the door shut as quietly as I could.

"Phew!" I whispered, leaning my head on the door and taking a huge sigh of relief. "I made it in."

Just then, I turned around to face the giant wall of video screens that displayed the feeds from all the cameras.

I looked up, only to see two of the meanest eyes I had ever seen glaring back down at me.

They were the eyes of Principal Tom Andrews!

2:09 p.m.

CHAPTER 22

2:10 p.m.

I jumped back in fear at the sight of Mr. Andrews towering over me with that look in his eye.

"Well, well," the principal taunted, "if it isn't Chase Manning, boy detective."

I had never seen this evil side of Mr. Andrews before. Earlier, I wasn't sure whether to believe Jenny's story about the principal's cruel comments to Mrs. Washington outside her office. Now I was experiencing the same treatment.

"Looking for this?" Mr. Andrews asked, dangling the videotape from the security camera in front of my face.

I didn't say a word.

"So you tracked me down, didn't you? Well, congratulations. Nice job, nice job," he said sarcastically.

"So, it *was* you!" I responded, finally confirming the identity of the thief.

"It was me, all right," he admitted. "But tell me, son, how did you track me down?"

"I just put the clues together."

"What clues would that be?" Mr. Andrews fired back.

"All your second place music awards, for starters. At lunch Coach Turner went on and on about how second place can make a person do strange things. It occurred to me that four second place finishes might even drive a principal to steal a cello."

"Very good, Chase. What else?"

"PE class. Coach Turner said you wanted us off the playground. I didn't think anything of it at the time. But then I realized that you probably needed us off the playground so you could go hide the cello someplace without anybody noticing."

"Boy, you *are* good," Mr. Andrews mocked. "Anything else?"

"I also know about the argument you had earlier with Mrs. Washington, where you wished her luck finding a new job and told her you knew you'd beat her sooner or later."

"Correct again. Anything else?"

"Yes, the clue that sealed the deal. I know about the phony raffle. I know you told Coach Turner to take me to lunch so I wouldn't be able to keep investigating. That's also why you had me investigate Brock, Dave, and Amy."

"That was brilliant, wasn't it?" he said, praising himself. "And don't forget poor, sweet Mrs. Washington. I actually had you thinking that *she* stole the cello."

"You must have wanted her out of here badly if you were willing to commit a crime to destroy the music program."

"Chase, you have no idea what it's been like for me these last few years. Finally I realize my dream of becoming a principal, and they send me *here*, to Apple Valley, where the woman who beat me four times is the music teacher. Every day that I see her is a heartbreaking reminder of my four losses. I couldn't take it anymore! Oh, how I can't stand that woman!"

I couldn't believe what was happening. Here was the principal in the security room, and he was actually confessing everything. I couldn't wait to go tell Jenny and Mrs. Kennedy. This was too good to be true.

"But, Chase, you've still got one big problem."

I had no idea what he was talking about.

"Everything you said is true," Mr. Andrews continued. "You've got powerful evidence against me. But here's the thing. You can't prove one bit of it."

I didn't know how to react to what I was hearing, but I could sense my bubble bursting.

Principal Andrews went on. "Chase, who's going to believe you? Remember, it's your word against mine. Sure, you've got a great reputation around here. But so do I."

I knew Mr. Andrews was right. I needed actual physical proof against the principal to go along with the rest of my evidence. Otherwise, it would be my word against his.

I just sat there, unsure of what to say or do next. I wanted to reach out and grab the videotape, but Mr. Andrews held it tightly in his hands.

As I tried to think of a new plan, Mr. Andrews took a lighter out of his pocket and held it up to the tape. The Principal started laughing uncontrollably. Then he set fire to the evidence.

I could do nothing but watch that tape burn into ashes right in front of my very eyes.

2:29 p.m.

CHAPTER 23

2:30 p.m.

As quickly as I could, I ran out of the security room and hustled back to class. On my way, I checked my watch. Only fifteen minutes until my tryout and a half hour until vacation. How was I going to solve this crime in such a short time?

Jenny returned from her tryout just as I approached the classroom door.

"How did your tryout go?" I asked, still bitter about her decision.

"It went fine. How did it go at the security room?"

"Not quite as well."

Mrs. Kennedy met us at the door the instant we made it inside. I think she could tell by looking at my face that for the second time in less than an hour, things hadn't gone as planned with Mr. Andrews.

I wanted to tell both of them all about what had just happened, but there wasn't time. I just said that Mr.

Andrews was in the security room when I got there, confessed to everything, and then burned the tape so there would be no physical evidence against him.

I was unbelievably frustrated at this point—at Jenny, at Mr. Andrews, at the rapidly disappearing minutes on the clock, and by the prospect of having to go to my tryout facing the very real possibility that I would be auditioning for an orchestra that soon wouldn't exist.

I tried to hide my emotions as best I could, so I put on a look of total determination. I would find a way to catch Mr. Andrews if it was the last thing I did.

As the three of us looked at one another, we knew we had to come up with something immediately.

"Without that tape, what other physical evidence against Mr. Andrews can we get?" Jenny asked.

"That's a good question," Mrs. Kennedy said. "But I'm not sure I have the answer."

"I do," I responded confidently.

"What?" inquired Jenny.

"It's come down to this," I said. "If we're going to catch this guy, then we need the cello."

The other two nodded in agreement.

"We know it's still here at school," I said. "All we have to do is track it down, and we've got him."

"But where could it be?" asked Mrs. Kennedy.

I then moved over to the window and surveyed the campus. Jenny and Mrs. Kennedy followed. I looked at my watch. My tryout was scheduled to start in three minutes. I felt as if a hundred butterflies were having a party in my stomach.

"That's strange," Jenny commented. "Coach Turner's having PE outside. Why did he make our class go into the auditorium for PE, but not this class?"

"Jenny," I corrected, "Coach didn't make us have PE in the auditorium. Mr. Andrews did."

Then, all of a sudden, I remembered my conversation with Mr. Andrews in the security room. The principal admitted that he told Coach Turner to get the kids off the yard so he could hide the cello somewhere without anybody noticing.

"But where could he hide it?" Mrs. Kennedy asked.

I studied the playground. That cello had to be somewhere out there. But where? I looked at my watch again. Two minutes until my tryout.

"Chase, you have to go now!" Jenny implored. "You can't miss your tryout! The honors orchestra has been your dream for years!"

"She's right, Chase. Don't worry about finding the cello now! Jenny and I will think of something. You need to leave!" Mrs. Kennedy said.

I needed to make a decision, right then.

"I can't do it! I can't leave now! I'm staying."

"But, Chase, you can't miss this opportunity! The music boosters and alumni who are conducting the auditions are only in town for one day! It's now or never!" Mrs. Kennedy said, grabbing me by the shoulders.

"I know, but I just can't let Mr. Andrews get away with this! I can't let him do this to Mrs. Washington. I'm staying."

Jenny had a look of sheer horror on her face. Mrs. Kennedy just stood there with her face in her hands, shaking her head from side to side.

I began to study the playground again.

Then, literally a second later, it hit me!

"I know! The ball box!" I announced.

"Yeah!" Jenny replied. "It has to be the ball box."

"Mrs. Kennedy, we have to go there right now!" I insisted.

"OK, we can go. I'll ask Mrs. Johnson next door to keep an eye on everybody else."

"Good idea," said Jenny. "Let's go."

"But wait!" Mrs. Kennedy directed. "There are three other people who should be there when we open the ball box. We need to go get them first."

"But, Mrs. Kennedy, we don't have time to round people up right now. We have to go!" I said.

"I wish there was a way I could call them on our way to the playground, but my phone is at home today," Mrs. Kennedy remembered.

"You can use my phone, Mrs. Kennedy," Jenny suggested.

"Jenny, you know you're not supposed to have a phone on campus during school hours."

"I know. It'll be just for today. I've heard cell phones can come in handy in situations like this," she said, barely able to contain her smile.

"Yeah," I added, giving Jenny a wink, "I've also heard cell phones can come in handy."

"Well, OK, this is an emergency. Go get it for me, Jenny, quickly," Mrs. Kennedy said.

And with that, Jenny and I scrambled to the door with our teacher, talking on the cell phone, close behind. We were heading straight for the ball box.

The moment of truth was now at hand.

2:46 p.m.

CHAPTER 24

2:47 p.m.

Mrs. Kennedy saw Coach Turner on the playground as the three of us approached the ball box. She called him over and asked him to open it for her.

Seeing that I was with her, the coach seemed to understand the reason for her request and said he'd be happy to help. He took out his keys and searched for the one that opened the ball box.

Just then, Mrs. Washington and Mrs. Simmons rushed over to join us.

"They must be two of the people that Mrs. Kennedy called," Jenny whispered to me.

Coach Turner located the key to the ball box. Jenny and I were getting very excited at this point. We knew it would be only a few seconds before the cello was revealed for all to see.

At that moment, I heard familiar footsteps coming

our way. "Oh, no!" I groaned, shaking my head after seeing who it was. "This guy is everywhere!"

Sure enough, none other than Mr. Andrews was hustling towards us.

"What's going on here? What's the meaning of this?" he asked sternly.

"Tom, you know exactly what's going on," Mrs. Kennedy responded sharply.

"Judy, I have no idea what you mean," the principal said with a straight face. "Now, I demand that all of you leave this area right away. School will be over in a few minutes and we must have the playground cleared."

"Why, so you can go hide the cello someplace else?" Mrs. Kennedy snapped back.

I had never seen this determined side of Mrs. Kennedy's personality before, but I liked it.

Just then, as Mr. Andrews was about to lash back at her, a police officer showed up.

I turned to Jenny. "And *that* must have been the third person she called on the phone," I whispered, beginning to smile.

"Excuse me," the man interjected. "My name is Officer Martin. What seems to be the trouble here?"

"Officer, I have everything under control," Mr.

Andrews said, trying to take charge. "You really aren't needed. We were all about to head back to our rooms. Why don't you just—"

"Officer, listen to me!" Mrs. Kennedy interrupted, pointing at Mr. Andrews. "That man stole a valuable cello this morning from its display case near the office and hid it in this ball box. We were just about to open it up when he came over to stop us."

"Is this true, sir?" Officer Martin asked, looking at Mr. Andrews.

"Absolutely not!" replied the principal. "As I was saying, we were all just heading back to our classes. Really, Officer, you're not needed here."

But Officer Martin wasn't going away so quickly. He looked at Mr. Andrews with an expression of deep concern. "That's a serious charge, sir. Certainly you don't mind if we open the ball box?"

"Why, no, Officer," Mr. Andrews said, suddenly backing down. "I have nothing to hide."

I couldn't believe that Mr. Andrews was lying right to Officer Martin's face. Any last bit of respect that I had for the man was gone.

Coach Turner stepped up and opened the ball box. There it was, right behind the Hula-Hoops.

The cello.

Jenny and I had never been so happy to see anything in our whole lives. Fortunately, it was unscratched and as beautiful as ever.

Mrs. Washington and Mrs. Simmons gave each other a big smile.

After seeing the cello, Principal Andrews put on the most innocent expression he could muster and said, "Officer, honestly, I'm as surprised to see that cello as anyone! I'm so happy that we found it! Now our auction tonight can proceed, and our instrumental music program can be saved!"

Officer Martin wasn't buying a word of it. "Sir, I think you better come with me."

"But wait!" Mr. Andrews said. "You can't arrest me. You have no evidence that I put that there!"

"Oh, please, Tom!" Mrs. Kennedy snapped. "We all know what you've been up to today."

"Oh, yeah? *What* do you know?" he said.

I began to wonder if the investigation was going to fall apart at this point. But justice would be denied no longer.

Coach Turner stepped up and said, "I know you asked me to take my class into the auditorium this morning because you didn't want anybody around when you hid that cello in here."

"But—" Mr. Andrews muttered, trying to protest.

"I know how upset you are about finishing second so many times in the music competition," Mrs. Kennedy interrupted.

"But—"

"I know about the argument you had with Mrs. Washington earlier where you wished her luck finding another job next year," Jenny added.

"But—"

"I know you made up three kids for me to investigate to throw me off your trail," I said.

"But—"

"And I know you faked the raffle and sent me to lunch with Chase," Coach Turner said.

"But—"

"And I know we're going to find a missing section from this morning's security tape," I said.

"But—"

"And I have an idea," Officer Martin said, "of whose fingerprints are going to be on that cello when I dust it in a minute."

Mr. Andrews knew that he had come to the end of the line. "OK, OK, enough already!" he shouted. "I admit it. I took the cello." He pointed at Mrs. Washington. "And I almost got rid of you once and for all!"

Calmly, I turned toward Officer Martin and said, "Officer, take him away." I had heard that on a TV show once and had always wanted to say it.

As Officer Martin led the principal away in handcuffs, everybody ran up to me and gave me a huge hug. They were ecstatic. Everyone except me.

Mrs. Simmons approached me and said, "Why, Chase, you saved our music program! We can't thank you enough for all you've done. Since you found the cello, your dream of being in the honors orchestra next year can come true after all."

"I'm afraid it can't," I replied.

"Whatever do you mean, dear?" she asked, confused.

"I didn't make it to my tryout, and Mr. Andrews said the other day that anybody who wanted to be in next year's honors orchestra had to try out by this afternoon. No exceptions. I'm happy that the other kids will get to play in the orchestra. Unfortunately, I just won't be able to join them."

"Never mind what that thief says! I'm the PTA president and I'm going to make an exception. After what you did today, there couldn't be a music program next year without you. You go practice right now, and I'll arrange a special tryout before tonight's Spring String Thing just for you."

I was so happy to hear that news, I reached over and gave Mrs. Simmons a nice fist bump. What the heck?

And with that, all seemed right with the world again. In a little while, everything and everybody would be exactly where they belonged.

The cello: safely behind the glass in the entryway.

Coach Turner: behind the wheel of his car, heading to the mountains with his family.

Me: behind my music stand practicing for tonight.

And Principal Tom Andrews: securely behind bars.

3:00 p.m.

Epilogue

The Spring String Thing was a smashing success. The entire Apple Valley community rallied to support our music program in fine style.

After our school's different orchestras each performed a few songs, the kids left and the parents, music boosters, community members, and out-of-town guests stayed for the dinner and auction.

George Wilson, a local businessman, outbid two other interested individuals and bought the cello for far more money than the school needed. In addition, the PTA sold more tickets to this event than ever before. So, combining the totals from the auction, ticket sales, and other related fund-raising efforts, the school raised enough money to keep the music program safe for the foreseeable future.

My day of firsts continued. I made history as the first student ever to attend Apple Valley's annual dinner and auction. Merely attend, I did not. The PTA invited me to be its guest of honor and stay for the entire event. I sat with my parents at the center table and watched the auction unfold before my eyes.

Once the auction concluded, Mr. Wilson walked up to the podium to claim the cello. After Mrs. Simmons congratulated him and handed over the cello, Mr. Wilson approached the microphone and said, "I'd like Chase Manning to join me on stage."

I was shocked to hear my name called and have everyone look at me while I still had dessert in my mouth.

I was also a bit embarrassed to have everybody applaud for me as I stepped to the podium. I couldn't be sure, but I think I was blushing.

"Mrs. Simmons, if you don't mind, I would like to say a few words," Mr. Wilson requested.

"Certainly," she replied. "Go right ahead." Considering the amount of money Mr. Wilson had just spent, I bet Mrs. Simmons would have been willing to name the school after him, let alone allow him to say a few words to the audience.

Mr. Wilson put his hand on my shoulder and looked out to the crowd. "Because of this young boy's courage and determination, Apple Valley Elementary will now be able to continue its award-winning music program for years to come. My own children played in the school's orchestras and had wonderful experiences. Music means a tremendous amount to my family, and I'm so pleased that I could be here this evening to lend a hand. Tonight, Chase, everybody in this room and every member of the Apple Valley community owes you a huge debt of gratitude."

Mr. Wilson's words brought even more applause.

Then Mr. Wilson turned and addressed me directly. "Now, Chase, they tell me you are looking forward to being in the Sixth Grade Honors Orchestra next year. Is that correct?"

"Yes, sir."

"And I understand Mrs. Simmons arranged a special tryout for you just a little while ago."

"Yes, sir. The committee said they'd let me know if I made it sometime after spring break."

"Well, Chase, I have a surprise announcement to share. You won't be needing to wait that long to find out."

What exactly did he mean?

"Chase, I'm delighted to tell you that the committee decided right after your tryout to make you a member of next year's honors orchestra."

"Wow, that's awesome news," I said, looking over at my smiling parents.

"I'm glad you think so, but I might actually be able to top it," Mr. Wilson continued.

"Sir?"

"You're playing the cello in this year's intermediate orchestra, is that right?"

"Yes, sir."

"A rented one?"

"Yes."

"Don't get me wrong, there's certainly nothing wrong with a rented cello, but I think the fellow who did what you did to save Apple Valley's music program should play something a bit nicer next year. Because of what you have done today, it is my honor to present you with this one."

Mr. Wilson then handed me the cello that I worked so hard to find, and the audience rose to its feet and gave both of us a standing ovation.

That night, with my new cello at my side, I had the best sleep I'd had in a long, long time.

About the Author

Steve Reifman is a National Board Certified Teacher, author, and speaker living in Santa Monica, California. *Chase Against Time* is the first installment in the Chase Manning Mystery Series. Be on the lookout for the next Chase Manning mystery, *Chase for Home.*

Steve has also written five resource books for teachers and parents, including *Changing Kids' Lives One Quote at a Time* and *Eight Essentials for Empowered Teaching and Learning, K–8.* You can find weekly teaching tips, blog posts, and other valuable resources and strategies for teaching the whole child at www.stevereifman.com. You can follow Steve on Twitter at www.twitter.com/#!/stevereifman.